I Shall Never Speak

A NOVEL BY

GINA V. KAIPER

THE DAYS & YEARS PRESS

PLEASANTON, CALIFORNIA

I Shall Never Speak is published by

THE DAYS & YEARS PRESS

P.O. Box 10667
Pleasanton, CA 94588
Tel: 510-463-0468
Fax: 510-463-0481

Printed in the United States of America
10 9 8 7 6 5 4 3 2 1

PUBLISHER'S CATALOGING-IN-PUBLICATION DATA

Kaiper, Gina V.

   I shall never speak/Gina V. Kaiper

ISBN-0-9645206-2-1

1. North Carolina—1775–1865—Fiction. 2. Folk art—American—Fiction. I. Title.

95-92027

Contents

Chapter One

Tuesday, November 6th, 1860

I shall never speak these thoughts to another living soul. Perhaps I shouldn't speak them now, but Ike is downstairs dying, and I want to sort things out and set the matter straight. I wish I could plead Ike's forgiveness, late as it is. After all these years of keeping my secret hid, I yearn to free myself of its burden, but simple kindness demands that I forbear. If I could not tell Ike years ago, then I must not tell him now, even were he pert enough to hear. No, this load is mine alone. Ike is passing through his own travail, and I mustn't add to his woes.

Isaac Howell is generous and loving to the core—I have never doubted that, and I hope to goodness I would not have married him, did I not believe it so. But would he understand, even now? Would he forgive me? Few men, or women either, can ever step aside from all the notions that bind them tight. So these thoughts and whispers shall mix with the dust in this attic. They'll lie here undisturbed for another spate of years, with only spiders to bear witness to what I say.

I have never been afraid of spiders. I guess I'm bolder than many women about a lot of things—and yet my cowardice crops up in unexpected ways. If I were truly bold—if I had spoken years ago—I would not be sitting here now, worrying over this secret.

One of Tom Yancey's Negroes was bit by a spider last month, a black widow, and his arm swelled up so bad that they had to saw it off. His right arm too. Tom was fit to be tied, losing the use of a good field Negro like that. Even if he sells that man now, he won't get back what he paid. I've heard tell a black widow will kill and eat her own mate, her own kin, and I reckon that's why the Lord Almighty chose to mark her so, with the sign of blood upon her breast, as warning. He did it, I suppose, for the exact same reason he placed a mark on Cain.

I have never understood why red is the color for evil and sin. Red is my favorite color. Oh, I like all the hues, but I'm always partial to red. I like red flowers, red birds, and red bonnets—but I reckon soon I'll lay my own red bonnet away in one of these trunks up here. It wouldn't look proper to wear bright silk atop my widow's weeds.

I am almost a widow. My husband is dying. I have to acknowledge that fact, though I'm not accustomed to it yet. Up here in this attic alone, with all my thoughts and memories, while Lydia sits by her daddy's sickbed below, I can picture Ike as hale as he's always been. It seems only yesterday that my brother James and my sister Caroline and me were walking through the evening on our way to singing school, and meeting Isaac Howell and his sister Rose-Ellen there. We were all of us young and laughing then. Has it been forty years already? Now Ike and me are the only ones left, and soon it will be just me.

"Mrs. Howell, I'd best advise you that it's only a matter of time," Doctor Riggs told me the other day. "I've tried every possible thing I know to do, and now I'm turning the case back over to Isaac's Maker. It could be next week, or next month—there's no real way to predict exactly."

Doctor Riggs says the sourness we've been smelling is one indication that Isaac Howell's earthly time is running out. It would bother Ike something fierce if he knew he smelled that way. Ike Howell has always been such a clean and handsome man.

I suppose I ought to be thankful, at least, that it's not still summertime, that the weather has cooled a considerable bit. And maybe it's a blessing too that Ike is not entirely clear to his mind. He sleeps most of the day, only waking now and again to whisper a word or two. It's because of all the poisons flowing through him, the doctor says.

The Isaac Howell of forty years ago—or even forty days ago—would be mortally embarrassed at what I now have to do. Help him to the chamber pot. Strip him down to his nakedness and bathe him once a day. Feed him broth and soup, instead of chicken and ham. I can hardly bear the sorrow, it tears at me so.

Every morning I roll him over to change the linen of his bed, and then I brush his hair and beard. Doctor Riggs advised me to have Ike's beard shaved away, but I refused. It would be too much. A man must have some pride, even when he's dying. Besides, I have always admired Ike's beard, rough and curly, the natural mark of a man. I even admired it way back then, when we were all going to singing school. I admire it still.

It was last Saturday evening when Doctor Riggs stopped in—or it may have been Sunday. The days blur, one into the other. I reckon it's because I've stayed cooped up in this house so long, sitting up every night with Ike and breaking all the patterns I've grown accustomed to.

But there's no mistaking today. It's Tuesday, for certain. Election Day. With all that hoopla and shouting in the streets down there, it couldn't be anything *but* Election Day. Ever since dawn, there've been wagons and mules passing this house and bringing folks in from the countryside. And the brandy's been flowing since dawn too, from the sound of things. By the time the frolicking is over, there'll be more than one voter, I expect, lying by the roadside and waiting to return to his senses again.

I just hope no one is hurt this year, more than a fist fight or such. A dozen times already I've heard the sound of a pistol or a gun. Of course, shooting is not unusual to hear around these parts. But all day long? Every few minutes or so? It's a wonder it hasn't disturbed Ike from his slumber, and in fact he did rouse up a while ago but sunk right down again.

Everyone is extra spirited this year, with all the disputing and declaring on every side of the fence. Some folks claim we should exercise our God-given right to secede, that we should have done it years ago, but others say no, that bad as it's gotten, it's not so bad as that. And of course there's always a few who have to talk big and swagger around. I expect it's one of those braggarts out there now, trying to prove he knows how to fire a gun. Well, pray to heaven it's just a squirrel or a jug he's out there shooting at—or even straight up in the air—and not at another human being. There hasn't been a duel in this county, that I've heard about, for a good half dozen years. I hope to never see such foolishness again.

Still, these are not normal times—even a woman can attest to that. Everywhere you look, folks are saying the most outrageous things. Why, just a week ago, five men came by this house—and two of Ike's close friends among them, I am ashamed to say. Naturally I assumed they'd come to inquire about my husband's state of health.

I said I knew he'd appreciate them dropping by, but that he happened to be asleep just then. Well, they appeared distressed by that information. I saw the looks they exchanged. So finally Rudy Nesbitt, who runs the cotton gin, said they apologized for asking it, but would I mind to wake my husband up? For only a few minutes, he said, just long enough for Isaac to sign his legal name.

I thought it was something important, something to do with Ike's store, or about his will and testament, until I realized that there wasn't a lawyer or a justice among them. And I *did* try to wake him up, but it was one of those times that Ike was plumb shed of his mind, and I never did succeed. We could not even persuade him to grasp the pen they thrust into his hand. Try as we would, his fingers kept slipping away, and the more we tried, the more agitated those men became.

Finally the truth came out. Those men had come to this house to get Ike's voting commitment. They wanted him to sign because they were fearful he might not even *last* until Election Day. Now doesn't that beat all? Can you believe the lengths some folks will go, without embarrassment?

Well, you can be sure that I showed those five gentlemen straight to the door, right then, and I haven't seen a one of them since. And you can also be sure that I haven't disturbed Isaac Howell about it, either. I reckon there's a number of things I won't be speaking to Ike about. If he's called to depart this life, I want him at least to go in peace— no matter how burdensome the silence that I must continue to keep.

I am not entirely certain who Ike would be voting for, were he up and about today. He used to be a Whig, but the Whigs aren't much in action any more. I imagine he'd go for Senator John Bell of Tennessee, or at least I hope he would, but there's so much back-and-forth this time that nothing's for certain. At any rate, few folks here in North Carolina will be choosing Mr. Abraham Lincoln.

But it does no good for me to sit here in this attic and speculate about what might have been. Before the sun goes down this day, things will have been determined, one way or another—but without Isaac Howell's assistance, this time around.

Heaven knows how long I've been sitting here, talking to myself this way, and letting my thoughts go wandering where they will. I'd best get on downstairs and spell Lydia for another turn. The shadows have grown so thick up here that I could not sign *my* legal name, even if I had a pen. *Mrs. Isaac Howell.* Will I still be that, once Ike has departed? Or *Mrs. Dorcas Howell?* What is the proper way for a widow to sign herself? I've never kept track of such things, but someone is bound to inform me before too long. Whichever, there's no way on earth I can ever go back to being young *Dorcas Reed* again.

Chapter Two

Wednesday, November 7th, 1860

Why do I feel so at home, sitting up here in this attic? I reckon it's because James and Caroline and me used to sleep in the loft at home, after we'd grown too big for the trundle bed. When Caroline and me were about to begin our womanhood—it was the same summer, I remember, that my sister Nancy died—our daddy partitioned up the loft to make a separate room for my brother James. It was the first time we'd been apart, James and Caroline and me. James was two years older than myself, and Caroline was two years younger. Like stairsteps, we were, but I was the fortunate one, the only one born in the exact same month and year that this century began. I used to consider that a sign that my life would turn out special, but of course I abandoned that notion several decades ago.

When I look out this attic window, I like to fancy I can see clear out to where our home place used to be. I tell myself that one of those tallest oaks, out yonder a mile or so, is the same oak tree that stood in our yard, halfway between the house and the stable. In summer, on the days when our daddy was smithing, he would set his forge in the shade of that tree, and we children would have to fetch springwater to fill the quenching barrel. On warm days, every task that could be transported we'd carry out to the porch or else to that tree—churning butter, snapping beans, and even spinning. We'd set the wheel on a bare-swept level spot. I remember once a cinder from Daddy's forge happened to land in the basket of flax, where it burned a considerable hole. I remember, too, the scolding I got for that.

Our house was built of puncheons, with two rooms and a passageway below, and then upstairs was our loft. That loft seemed enormous to me then, before our daddy put the partition in, but I doubt it was half the size of this attic here. This town wasn't even founded back then. That came later, with the railroad. When we were living to home, there were only a half dozen houses scattered within hollering distance of where the Fayetteville fork branched from the stage road to Raleigh.

That old puncheon house caught fire and burned to the ground some few years after James and Caroline and me had sold it off. By then, Caroline was married and living next to Ike's store, and James and Rose-Ellen and me had moved down to Fayetteville. I didn't see it burn, and I've always been grateful for that.

I slept in at attic too, down in Fayetteville, right over the family wing where James and Rose-Ellen had their quarters. I painted that room myself, the color of cream, and then I stenciled a row of bright red berries below the eaves all around. That gave me great satisfaction. It was a small room, but I can truthfully say that I've never had a place I liked so much as that, not even here in this house, where I've had full liberty to do and fix as I please. No, that little room was special. I kept my easel set up there.

It's peculiar, I suppose, that a person as tall as me should be partial to attics where I can't even stand up straight, except directly beneath the ridge. I took my height from my daddy. He was a strapping man, and my brother James was tall too, though he never achieved the girth or strength that I associate with Daddy. Of course, James never took up smithing. Both my brother and Isaac Howell stood almost equal in height. They each were slightly more than six feet tall—about a hand's breadth taller than me. We measured once, I remember, all of us.

My height has given me endless pain and embarrassment over the years, though I'm mostly reconciled to it now. A young woman is judged by the beaux she has, and it's a grievous thing to stand taller than half the men you know. I used to pray fervently for a miracle that would shrink me down to a more becoming size—more like Caroline. Caroline resembled Mama, both of them considerably shorter than me.

I can't remember whether Nancy, my older sister, was short like Caroline or whether she was tall like me. I suppose that's because Nancy always seemed big to me. By the time I was eleven, she was already married and living some fifteen miles away. Nancy died in childbed the summer I was twelve, and the baby died too. I don't think Mama ever forgave herself for not being on hand when the birthing commenced, but it came on sudden, so another midwife had to be called instead. Besides, there's no way of knowing that things would have ended different, even if Mama had been there.

For the longest time after that, I was taunted with notions of giving birth to a child. It seemed to me the bravest thing a woman could ever do, to walk through the Valley of the Shadow of Death and bear all that suffering and pain, for the sake of generating another human creature. I was still young enough to be innocent of certain specifics, but I let my imagination take full rein and would lie awake at night, torturing myself with all the terrible sensations that would attend when *my* time came to be delivered. I'd actually writhe and moan, and bite my lips to keep from crying out and waking Caroline beside me.

For years, I dreaded childbirth more acutely than anything—and yet, at the same time, I was terribly eager to be tested. I wanted to prove myself equal to whatever dangers might arise. All that wasted worry. Childbirth is one experience I've never been called upon to face.

My mama was the midwife in our neighborhood. As early as I can remember, folks would appear at our door, sometimes in the middle of the night, to say that so-and-so had just took sick, and would Mama mind to come. Childbirth, illness, and death—everyone called on Mama. Back then, the closest doctor lived a three hours' ride away, so Mama would have to rely on her own best judgment, most of the time.

I don't recall Mama ever refusing a plea for help, especially after Caroline and me had gotten big enough to take her place in fixing dinner for Daddy. Mama kept a special apron and a plain linen cap to wear on such occasions. Sometimes she'd be gone for two or three days, if the folks lived far, but most times she'd come home at nightfall and leave again at dawn, doing whatever was needed. And then after the person was recovered—or dead, either one—Mama would fire up her washpot in the yard, and she'd boil that apron and cap, and her dress and petticoats too, for a good long while. It was the only washing where me and Caroline weren't required to help.

My sister Nancy's death was the first tragedy I personally ever experienced—but not the last. Four years later we lost Mama. It was early September, fiercely hot, and there was fever in the neighborhood. Mama was sent for, to nurse one of the Lattimore boys, one of the twins, and while she was there, the other one came down too. One of those boys died, and the other one lived, and altogether Mama was gone for most of a week.

When she came home, it was already evening. Not quite dark, but the lightning bugs were beginning to flicker. We'd eaten supper, the four of us, and Caroline and me were washing up when we heard Mr. Lattimore's wagon pull into the yard. Mama didn't say anything to James or Caroline or me but called straight out for Daddy.

"Jacob!" she said. "I need to talk to you!"

The cart departed, and Daddy and Mama stood talking for a piece beneath the oak tree. I couldn't hear a word they said, but pretty soon Daddy came back to the house and asked for our assistance. We helped him clear everything out of the downstairs room where he and Mama slept—everything except the bed, a table, and one straight-backed chair. The braided hearth rug, the quilt chest, and even Mama's Sunday bonnet were carried upstairs to our loft, and then I swept the room while Caroline fixed the bed, and all this time Mama was sitting out in the dark, out beneath the tree, apparently paying us no mind. And when we were done, Daddy told James and Caroline and me to go on upstairs, but he said for us to pray that night like we'd never prayed before.

"All right, Sarah!" we heard Daddy call. "Everything's ready—we've done exactly what you said!"

And then we heard Mama come into the house, and the bedroom door was shut. That door was still closed the next morning when I came downstairs. Mama was ill, and Daddy had sat up watching over her all night, and he stayed right with her all that day. We weren't allowed to help him, me and James and Caroline, outside of doing our regular chores, except that Daddy requested James to feed the horses in his stead. Then, late in the afternoon, Daddy called to us, and directed us to stand just outside the bedroom door. We peered in to where Mama lay on the bed, her hair every which way. Daddy wiped her face and held a dipper of water to her lips, and Mama whispered something, but we couldn't make out what.

Daddy straightened up and said, "She says she hopes to heaven you'll always be a credit to the way she's raised you up."

When I tried to step closer, Daddy shook his head.

"No, Dorcas! You stay just where you're at! I know you mean to be kind, but I intend to honor every jot and tittle your mama has said! Because I gave her my solemn promise, and I've never broken a promise to your mama."

Another few hours, and Mama was plumb incoherent, and she wouldn't eat or drink. Daddy stayed right by her side, scarcely eating himself, and before the week was out, our mama had departed this life.

Daddy laid her out himself—James and Caroline and me were not permitted to cross the threshold of that room, not even then. We could not look at our own mama, lying in her coffin, except from a distance of seven paces or so. We could not kiss her cheeks one final time, though Daddy did take the blossoms I'd gathered and fix them gently around her before he nailed on the lid.

She was buried by noon of the following day. Then Daddy himself, still refusing our help, dragged Mama's featherbed out to the middle of the yard, the bed that was her pride, and both of the bedpillows too. He built a whopping fire right there, and he burnt that bed and all the covers clean down to ashes, and Mama's apron and her linen cap, and even the gourd dipper where he'd given her to drink. It was hot as the dickens that afternoon, and then that terrible fire blazing up. I wondered had Daddy turned loose of his mind.

That finished, Daddy took a bucket of water and some lye soap and scrubbed the room where Mama had died, every inch of it, and the bedstead and table too. I shall never, as long as I live, forget the sight of my great big strapping daddy, down on his hands and knees, scrubbing that bare pine floor, and I couldn't tell whether it was tears or sweat dripping from his face.

And when it was over, Daddy took to bed himself. We were certain he'd caught the fever too, but it was grief instead. In three days he was up again, and tending to his horses, but it was a considerable while before he got to where he could laugh, or could even speak Mama's name aloud without his voice breaking.

I think of Mama so often as I sit downstairs beside Ike's bed. I wish I had half her patience, her fortitude and skill. I have wondered a dozen times, if she were here nursing Ike, what she'd advise me to do. Of course, Doctor Riggs stops by every two days or so. He's a smart and studying man, and he sends up North for all the latest potions to try. They don't bleed and purge much any more, the way they used to. Doctor Riggs says it's not the modern way. And this is not one of those scourges that carries so many folks away. Ike's is a private suffering, the doctor says. It is one man's bodily failure.

So be thankful, I tell myself, that Ike's misery can't be passed along to destroy someone else. I wish I could take more solace in that.

Chapter Three

Thursday, November 8th, 1860

Dan, Ike's oldest son, and his cousin Tom Yancey stopped by yesterday evening to bring us the election news. It appears that the Democrat, Mr. John C. Breckenridge of Kentucky, has carried this state, like folks expected, and yet it's Mr. Abraham Lincoln who's to be the next President. Dan and Tom said everyone's a-buzz since the word arrived yesterday noon on the lightning telegraph.

Some people claim that Abraham Lincoln is Satan in disguise—a spiteful, cunning man who aims to destroy us, one way or another. But other folks say that's to give him too much credit, because Abraham Lincoln is nothing but a rustic fool who hasn't got sense enough to see he's being dangled by a bunch of rich Yankees. Either way, everyone agrees that this turn of events can do us nothing but harm.

I don't know much about Mr. Lincoln myself. I've heard he can split a decent fence rail, though what that has to do with being President, I cannot imagine, since I doubt they're planning to put a split-rail fence around the White House, up to Washington City—though maybe it would be an improvement if they did.

My daddy was good at splitting fence rails too. We had a rail fence around the pasture that bordered on the stage road—that's where Daddy kept his horses. Daddy raised horses, in addition to smithing and working the farm. He never did grow much cotton, but I reckon his horses sufficed for a cash crop instead. There were always six or seven out in that pasture, as long as I can remember, and every spring there'd be one or two new foals, the dearest creatures you ever saw. I used to dread Court Week and Election Day, because that's when Daddy would take his horses off to trade. I can remember him riding off, with whichever mare or stallion he'd chosen tied to his saddle and trotting along behind. It would be a sad day for James and Caroline and me, because we knew we'd never see Knight or Beauty or Lucky Foot again.

Occasionally, folks would come right to the house to trade, looking for a fast mare to ride about, or a solid horse to hitch to their carriage or cart.

My daddy wouldn't trade with just everyone, though. I remember once, the spring after Mama died, there was a certain young gentleman came by and wanted a chestnut stallion that Daddy had then—a spirited horse, and a handsome one. The gentleman was handsome too, as I recall, and gracious as you please. He stood there chatting with me and Caroline, but mostly he wanted that horse, and wanted it something fierce. He offered my daddy one hundred dollars flat, but Daddy refused. Then he said a hundred and fifty, but Daddy said no. He even went clear to two hundred, but our daddy still shook his head. Then what *would* it take, he demanded.

"Well, sir," my daddy replied, "I don't figure on trading that horse today, so it don't matter *how* much you're willing to spend. If you're wanting a horse so bad, you'd best look somewheres else."

So that gentleman rared off, raising the dust behind him. Caroline and me were astounded. Two hundred dollars was a lot of money in those days—and still is. But once my daddy had made up his mind on a matter, he would not budge a quarter-inch.

"If he treats his animals as bad as he treats his Negroes," Daddy said, "then he don't deserve to own a horse. And he certainly ain't going to own any horse of mine!"

My daddy never owned a Negro. He would never even hire one for a few days' help, unless that man was free. For our daddy, it was a matter of principle. He didn't hold truck with slavery—I heard him proclaim as much a dozen times, sitting by the fireside with one of the neighbors, or talking politics while he forged a tool or a wheel. Of course, back then a man didn't have to be so fearful of stating his views on the matter. I guess it's just as well that Daddy never lived to see how things have turned out.

It was the Quaker in him, I suppose. Both Daddy and Mama were raised up Quakers in their youth, but they'd left it behind when they married. Daddy's folks plain disowned him for quitting the fold, but Mama's family had more compassion, because I can remember Grandmama Lacey coming to visit every once in a while. At any rate, by the time that James and Caroline and me came along, Daddy and Mama had both set their feet along the Methodist road. I don't know exactly when they converted, but I expect it was at some revival that swept through the neighborhood. Anyway, as long as I can remember, we were all connected to Emmaus Chapel, a small log meeting house that used to stand a few miles south of here. The Howells belonged there too, so we'd always see Ike and Rose-Ellen and their older sister Belle, whenever a preacher rode through and a service could be held.

Back then, Methodists didn't hold with slavery either— or at least some of them didn't—but of course that's all

16

changed now. So many things have changed. That old log chapel is gone, and we have a framed-in church house now, with a tower to hold the bell. We had that bell made special, up North somewhere.

I reckon my brother James and me inherited our slavery views from Daddy, like we did his height. I think we always held that slavery was shameful and wrong. And just like Daddy, whenever James needed to hire someone, he'd look for a man who was free, although once, down to Fayetteville, he did take on a stableman and cook, a man and his wife, whose owner had granted permission for them to hire out and buy themselves free. Back then, it was still possible to do that sometimes. I don't know if it was exactly legal, even then, but the laws weren't always so strictly regarded. Folks weren't so careful back then. Today, of course, that man and his wife would not be permitted to buy themselves free.

When Daddy died, the month after I turned eighteen, James hired a man named Free Jack to look after our horses whenever he was on the road. James had himself a job, carrying the mail to Fayetteville. Twice a week, he'd meet the stage coming west along the road to Raleigh, and he'd take the satchel of mail and head straight out for Fayetteville. Then, after resting his horse overnight, he'd pick up another packet and come home in time to meet the east-bound stage.

It was a good job for James. He had a horse that he was immensely proud of—in fact, it was that same chestnut stallion that Daddy had refused to sell. Daddy gave that horse to James specifically for the mail-riding job.

James was paid in cash, not trade. I don't know what he earned, but I doubt it was all that much. Maybe it even varied, depending on how many items he carried each time. James wasn't but nineteen when he started riding the mail, but Daddy let him keep all his wages, nonetheless. Every month James would slip a few coins into an old cracked pitcher that we kept on the mantel shelf—I had fixed a bouquet of dried posies in that same pitcher, so's to hide the money.

James was careful with money, even then, but every once in a while he would bring back something special from down to Fayetteville, something we couldn't buy at Mr. Howell's store. I'll never forget the day that James brought me my first set of watercolor paints, and seven sheets of real paper. Dorcas Reed was one elated girl that afternoon! Up to then, I'd had to make my own colors, by grinding rocks or berries to mix with eggwhite and whey. I was always experimenting, concocting my paints one way or another, and the same thing with my dyes. Nowadays, with factory cloth, we take bright colors for granted—or at least here in town we do—but back then we mostly relied on sumac and indigo.

Anyway, James enjoyed his mail-riding job, and the rest of us delighted in it too. There wasn't a newspaper published in this county back then, and of course there wasn't such a thing as the lightning telegraph—I doubt it had even been thought of. For news, we depended mostly on folks passing through, so it was plenty exciting to have my own brother riding off to Fayetteville two times a week. If ever a person was meant to live in town, it was my brother James. I reckon he thanked his lucky stars when that mail-riding job came along and Daddy consented for him to do it.

When Daddy died, James had been riding the mail for a year or so, and some of our neighbors thought that he ought to give it up. They said he oughtn't to ride off so far and leave me and Caroline alone. Folks said Free Jack would rob us blind, or maybe worse. But James knew what he was doing, and we never had any trouble. James let Free Jack farm a few of our acres in exchange for seeing to the horses. Of course James wasn't gone but two nights a week, and the rest of the time he could see to matters himself, so it worked out fine. We went on together that way for three or four years after the passing of our daddy.

I reckon I just assumed we would go on forever, the three of us living at home. But if there's one thing I've learned in the past sixty years, it's that changes will come whether you expect them or not. Someone will die, or there'll be a new road cut through, or another invention will appear. No matter how hard you try, you can never anticipate what those changes will be, not entirely.

Who would have thought that today we'd be receiving election news by the lightning telegraph? Or that someone named Abraham Lincoln would be chosen President—and that folks would be talking secession and war on account of it? Why, back when James was riding the mail, Abraham Lincoln was just a skinny little boy, off in the mountains somewhere.

And there's something else I've learned. Call it wisdom if you will, but it's my notion that for every lightning telegraph that comes along, you're just as likely to get a setback or a plague. Nothing guarantees that a change will turn out good. In fact, in my experience, it often falls the other way.

So I sit here in this attic, while Ike lies dying below— but try as hard as I can, I cannot ascertain what lies out yonder ahead.

Chapter Four

Friday, November 9th, 1860

I supposed I ought to feel ashamed, sitting up here idle for such a spell each afternoon, and yet it soothes my mind and helps me gather strength for staying by Ike's bedside yet another day. Folks take comfort different ways. Some cry, and some pray. Many times, these past decades, I have helped some poor bereaved woman console herself by piecing together a mourning quilt. Yet, when my turn comes, I hide up here in this attic. I sort not scraps of cloth but all these memories.

Mourning pictures were the style when I was younger. I embroidered one for Mama, with weeping willows above a pale blue stream. And after Daddy died, I worked up another to match. We hung the pair of them in our front room, and when James and Rose-Ellen and me moved down to Fayetteville, Caroline kept those mourning pictures here. I don't know where they are now.

Belle Yancey, Ike's older sister, liked those pictures so much that when her mother-in-law departed, old Mrs. Yancey, Belle asked would I mind to embroider one for her. Naturally I obliged, and in the next two or three years, I must have stitched mourning pictures for half the deceased from Emmaus Chapel. No two were exactly alike—I made a book of sketches, so I could keep track of them all. Every once in a while I come across one of those pictures I did back then, but they look old-fashioned to me now.

Belle Yancey did well for herself when she married. Her husband, Will, already owned five Negroes, and then he inherited a dozen more from his daddy. The Yanceys raised cotton from the first, and prospered with it. Belle and Will lived about four miles southwest of here, and Tom, their son, lives there yet. Tom still raises cotton—and still prospers. Just lately he built another wing onto the old house.

Belle would ask for my assistance right often in those years when James and Caroline and me were living here by ourselves. I have always been handy with a needle, ever since I can remember, and I've always had a good eye for colors too. Back in those early years, I would often get called upon to help with sewing one thing or another—mourning pictures, wedding quilts, baby clothes.

At first I did it just for the pleasure. I liked to sew, and I enjoyed getting out of the house and mingling with other folks. With plain folks, like us, it was a way of being neighborly, and it usually worked out to an even swap. I'd help someone piece a quilt or make a bonnet, knowing that they'd be willing to do the same for me.

But before long, it seemed like most of my time was spoken for by women like Belle Yancey and her friends—folks who weren't likely to offer me turn-about. Belle would send me word that she'd just acquired some new French calico, or a length of silk, and would I help her stitch it up? So I would take one of our horses and set out as soon as my chores were done to home, and sometimes Caroline would come with me too, and we'd stop for Rose-Ellen as well.

Caroline and Rose-Ellen both could sew a fine seam—
I doubt there's a woman in this county who can't sew a
proper seam—but Belle always made it clear that it was
my assistance she wanted when it came to cutting the garment out. Belle would describe what she had in mind—
maybe some frock she'd seen—and I would try to sketch it
out with pen and ink. Then she could say, no, the skirt was
fuller here, or the bodice was thus-and-so, and I'd alter my
drawing until she was satisfied.

The challenge came in cutting the pieces to match the
picture I'd made, and then in fitting the dress to Belle herself. Sometimes it took a bit of doing. I remember once I
spent an entire afternoon figuring how to fold a piece of
satin into an acceptable rose.

When Caroline and Rose-Ellen were both there, it was
almost like we were having a party. At noontime we'd stop
for dinner, and Belle would serve us tea in the china cups
that had belonged to old Mrs. Yancey. I doubt even Belle
Yancey used china cups for everyday, or drank tea either,
but she knew it would give us pleasure. Belle didn't have
to do her own cooking and washing up. One of the Negroes took care of that, and tended the children too.

I have to give Belle Yancey her due. She was fortunate
in her marriage, but she never put on airs, like many folks
do. Not that the Howells were paupers exactly. Ike's daddy
kept the store in our neighborhood, though back then it
didn't carry much, just coffee and axeheads and such.

With marriage, Belle seized an opportunity, that's all,
and she worked hard at learning the proper way to act.
She was a natural-born beauty and that helped. It was always a pleasure to make her a dress, knowing she'd do it
proud. Belle was seven or eight years older than me, but
she always treated me well, even before we had reason to
know we'd ever be kin.

I cannot say the same for every lady I sewed for back then, though they were seldom pure-out rude. Mostly they were thoughtless and vain, making assorted distinctions to be certain that I kept to my rightful place, though of course I was never in doubt. I knew I wasn't rich, and I wasn't a beauty. Who ever heard of a beauty as tall as me? But folks can devise an amazing array of signs to mark who is better than whom.

Looking back, I sometimes wonder why I ever consented to ride about the countryside that way, helping first one and then another sew up all those frocks for wearing to fancy parties that a person like me would never attend. Well, I do know why I did it—and if I'm honest, I'll admit that I'd do it all over again. I did it for the exact same reason that my brother James enjoyed his mail-riding job: because there was a certain satisfaction in sewing for someone who'd been to Raleigh or Wilmington, or maybe even as far as Charleston—or, if they hadn't traveled there themselves, at least they might have talked to folks who had.

And then there was the pleasure of working with the fabrics themselves—fabrics that had come from up North somewhere, or from England, and occasionally from France. I took a particular delight in silk, as bright as a butterfly's wing.

Besides, it was always understood that I'd have my pick of the leavings from any garment I helped to make, and at first it was enough to spend half a week helping one of Belle's friends make herself a frock, just for the sake of bringing home a scrap of silk the size of a dinner plate. Naturally I always shared with Caroline, even halves, because the more I helped other folks with their sewing, the more my sister Caroline had to tend to matters at home. Not that she ever objected, sweet-tempered soul that she was.

I made both me and Caroline bonnets as fine as any woman's in the county, trimmed with my scraps of ribbon and lace. We'd wear those pretty bonnets whenever there was preaching at Emmaus Chapel. Some folks said it was sinful to flaunt ourselves before the Lord that way, but we didn't pay much heed to that.

And of course we both worked mightily on our own wedding quilts. Flower Garden, Whig Rose, Tree of Life, and various complicated patterns that I would devise. If ever two young women aimed to be prepared for proper housekeeping when our turn came, it was Caroline and me. Naturally I assumed that I too would have need of such things, just as much as Caroline.

I am trying to recall, as I sit here now, exactly when I first began to sew for hire. I mean for actual coins, not just scraps of cloth. I believe it was a few months after Daddy died. Mrs. Florence Yates and her daughters came by the house in their carriage, wanting me to make them a set of traveling clothes. They were going up to Richmond for some reason that I now forget, perhaps to escape the vapors we used to fear back then.

It was clear that the sewing they had in mind would take more than a day or two. The first of our vegetables were coming in, I do remember that, and I had considerable work to do at home—so I declined. I said I was sorry, but I couldn't spare the time just then.

Lo and behold, Mrs. Florence said if I *could* arrange to make her frocks, she'd be eternally obliged...*and* she'd pay me forty pence a day besides.

Well! Imagine! Me, Dorcas Reed, earning forty pence a day! I reckon I never stopped to think that paying wages is one decisive way of distinguishing who is better than whom. Because the minute I accepted those coins, I bore the taint of trade. It wasn't a question any more of sewing just for the pleasure, or of doing someone a favor, even if I knew it wasn't likely that the favor would ever be returned.

It was plumb selfishness, I admit, but my first thought was to figure how many sheets of store-bought paper that forty pence would buy, and how many more watercolor paintings I could do as a consequence. By then, I had used up the paper that James had brought me from Fayetteville, and I hated to ask him for more. I had tried making paper myself, out of rags and cotton lint, but the experiment had not been entirely satisfactory. The texture was not the same.

Forty pence a day. So I invited those ladies into our front room and went to find my workbasket and my measuring tape, and that was that. Before many more weeks had passed, I would seldom consent to sew for anyone unless there *were* forty pence involved, although naturally I still did occasional favors for my friends. I was even so persnickety that I wouldn't take goods for trade. No hams or honey for Miss Dorcas Reed. No, thank you! Didn't we already have sufficient hams to home? And the amazing thing, as I was quick to learn, is that certain ladies will pay most anything to have their satin roses made and their flounces arranged in the most becoming way.

Soon, steady customers began finding their way to our house, and it wasn't long before I had my own penny jug sitting on the mantel. And I kept myself well supplied with store-bought paper and watercolor paint.

Chapter Five

Saturday, November 10th, 1860

A bird up over my head somewhere is singing his heart out. Whether he's on the roof or the chimney, I can't quite tell, but I have opened the window a crack, the better to hear. It's a wonderful song, full of trills and joy. He has to be singing for the pleasure, or else he'd never keep on so long. I wonder what that bird has to be singing about, this November afternoon. I hold my breath and listen, grateful for whatever songs find their way to cheer me these somber days.

Maybe that bird is singing the praise of his Maker. *Make a joyful noise unto the Lord, all ye lands! Serve the Lord with gladness! Come into His presence with singing!* That's a Psalm we used to sing, back in our singing school days, but I forget how the tune goes now. It was some old-time melody that you don't hear much any more.

I can't remember whose idea it was that the young folks of Emmaus Chapel should get together and sing each Friday evening. I expect it was Mr. Howell, Ike's daddy, since he was the one who spelled the hymns whenever we had services. All the Howells could sing. My brother James had a right good voice too, and so did Caroline, but my own particular talents have never lain in a musical way. Still, I could usually hold the tune, if someone else was carrying it along.

Anyway, we started our singing school the next year after Daddy had died. I remember being glad that our mourning time had passed so that me and James and Caroline could participate too. I reckon it's proper to sing the Lord's praises even in mourning, but we'd usually go on to more frolicking tunes, after we'd done with the hymns. And after we'd sung ourselves out, we'd eat melon or nuts or cake, whatever was to hand.

There were a few folks in the neighborhood who complained about us having such laughing good times, and about the young ladies mixing right in with the men. They said Emmaus Chapel ought not to sponsor such frivolity, but most folks considered it a wholesome thing. Wasn't it better to have us singing harmony and eating gingercake than running off somewhere to dance? Wasn't dancing much the graver sin?

My, how I used to look forward to those Friday evenings! It was then I first took notice of Isaac Howell as someone more than merely my brother's friend. I was nineteen and taking stock of every man in the neighborhood—that is, every man who was single, white, and under the age of thirty-five. There weren't a great many.

But there *was* Isaac Howell, smiling and handsome, with his curly brown beard and deep bass voice that sounded so fine. I could find no fault with Isaac Howell. To my knowledge, he didn't curse or drink liquor or bet on horses. And wasn't he honest and kind?

My awareness of Ike came not in one blinding flash but blossomed gradually. If Isaac Howell was anywhere in the vicinity, I knew it. I grew attuned to his presence in a physical way, like a sunflower, always turning to face the light. At Emmaus Chapel, even as I bowed my head and closed my eyes, thoughts of Isaac Howell would slyly entwine themselves into my prayer, no matter how earnest and penitent I meant to be. And on Friday nights, of course, I could always discern Ike's voice beneath the others. How sweet the sound!

I seldom lacked for occasions to see him because the five of us—Ike and his sister Rose-Ellen, and James and Caroline and me—always went together to singing school. If we had far to go, James would hitch up our wagon, but mostly we'd walk. And if our gathering had been at the Howells' place, which it frequently was, then James and Caroline and me would stay after everyone else had left, and we'd help wash up and set things straight. Sometimes James and Ike would get to talking politics with Mr. Howell, while the three of us girls helped Ike's mother wash the cups and sweep the floor. And often we'd take to singing again. Ike and Rose-Ellen, James and Caroline would harmonize together, and I'd sing too, but softly, so's not to spoil the sound.

Ike helped his daddy in the store. I guess they took turn-about: one in the store and one in the fields. I am ashamed to admit how many excuses I devised for visiting that store. I ran out of needles and pins faster than any seamstress in the state, and the worst of it was, I could have had my brother procure them down to Fayetteville—better pins, and cheaper too—but I didn't. No, I would head for the store on the least pretext, and sometimes Mr. Howell was there, and sometimes—praise the Lord!—it was Ike. He'd wait on me and inquire to things at home, and of course I'd ask after Rose-Ellen and his mama.

"Well, I reckon I'll see you-all on Friday night," he'd say.

I'd leave that store a-glow and walk home singing all the way, tuneful or not, I didn't care. Hadn't I talked to Ike, and hadn't he smiled at me? But I kept my affections a secret and never said a word about it to another living soul. Some folks can parade their feelings about, but not me. I keep things locked away—else why am I sitting here in this attic now, musing over a secret that I should have revealed long ago?

When I look back now, that whole year seems to be made of gold, just like that bird's song overhead. And then one afternoon, the summer I was twenty, one Saturday afternoon, Ike and James had been off fishing together and had come back to home. They were sitting on our front porch, sharing a cantaloupe between them, and I was sewing inside, with my chair pulled close to the open window and my heart a-flutter on account of Ike being so near.

They were talking about some trouble old Pinckney Smith was having with his hogs, when abruptly, almost in mid-sentence, Ike caught his breath and headed off in another direction.

"James," he said, "there's something mighty important that I been wanting to speak about, and I reckon now's as good as any other time."

"Well, I'm sitting here with both my ears attached," my brother James replied. "So go ahead and get it off your mind."

I leaned as close to the window as I dared. I know I should have tiptoed away, but rank curiosity has always been one of my traits. Besides, anything concerning Ike I wanted to know

"Course, if your daddy was alive," Ike said, "I'd be speaking directly to him. I want to do the right thing."

There was silence for a moment. Ike was mumbling so that it was all I could do to hear.

"I'm twenty-two, aren't I?" Ike said. "The same as you, a full-grown legal man, and Daddy's been paying me wages for the past year or more. It's not a lot, I realize, but he's

29

worked it out to give me the twenty-five acres just south of the store. I've got me a right good stand of oats this year, and some wheat that's coming along. Well, I don't need to repeat what you already know—it's just that...."

He paused, then proceeded again.

"Heck-fire, James—it's just that I got me a notion to take up courting with Caroline!"

Caroline! It's a wonder I didn't drop my scissors, or tip my chair and crash to the floor, I was that shocked and astounded—but I didn't. Instead, I sat right there, my hands shaking, my heart quivering, and heard the rest of it. If anyone had come into the room just then, I could not have spoken a word, not the faintest whisper.

"Has Caroline expressed herself?" James said.

"No, she hasn't. Not exactly. It's only a feeling I have, but somehow I doubt she'd mind."

"Well, then you'd best go to it," my brother James said, "because you won't ever hear an objection on my account."

So that was that, and before long it was Ike and Caroline, Ike and Caroline. Soon they were making their plans, and Ike had started building a two-room house on his land, about fifty yards from the store. My sister Caroline was plumb ecstatic, and the light of love shone clear upon her face. I don't know why I'd never noticed it before.

I was glad, then, that I had never let on to my foolishness, else I'd have likely died from embarrassment. There's pain and mortification enough in not being the chosen one, without having everyone's pity too. I can truthfully say that Caroline, bless her soul, never suspected a thing—and she died still innocent—because from that same Saturday afternoon, when I sat there hearing what I shouldn't, I took stern measures with myself. If Ike Howell belonged to Caroline, then it would be a sin and transgression for me to keep picturing him in my mind, even the slightest bit.

Was it love I felt for Isaac Howell, back then? A faint precursor to the love I feel for him now? I've asked myself that a dozen times over the past years, but each go-round I come to the same conclusion: no, it wasn't love, or anything like it. My affixment to Isaac Howell was only the silly notion of a girl who had been no place and had done nothing of consequence. It was a foolish empty notion, and that's all.

Of course, that's not to claim that I didn't grieve and pout at having to give that notion up. I am ashamed to admit it, but all the rest of that summer I seemed to develop a headache whenever Ike Howell would come to call on Caroline. For a time I lost all interest in going to singing school. I'd make up some excuse about how much sewing I'd promised to do, but the minute the others left the house, I'd lay my sewing aside and get out my watercolor paints, and I'd set to work by the light of a tallow candle.

Painting was the one thing that could lift my spirits and distract me from the bitterness that I mired in for a while. Painting freed my soul and gave me hope again. I would sketch the picture out and arrange it to suit my fancy, and then I would find great pleasure in dipping my brush into a pool of color and spreading that hue upon the paper. My own life might be murky and constrained, but green was always green, and red was always red, and there's such a purity in that.

I painted a whole series of Bible tales during the next six or seven weeks, when Ike was first beginning his courting of Caroline. I painted Sarah laughing at the Lord, and I painted the adulteress who spoke to Jesus—I tried to make her fetching in a way that I was not. And then I painted three or four versions of Jacob meeting Rachel at the well. For some reason, Caroline took a fancy to one of those Rachel pictures and begged me for it. Caroline liked all the paintings I did—she'd exclaim over every detail—but it's always seemed uncanny to me that Caroline should choose that one picture to hang above the bed where she and Ike slept. That same painting was hanging over her when she died. In fact, it's still in the upstairs hall, where I moved it after I took hold of the housekeeping here. Every once in a while, even now, I stop and look at that picture, and it puts me in mind of that painful time. Somehow, it makes me ashamed of myself, all over again.

Fortunately, though, it wasn't long before I grew accustomed to the sight of Ike and Caroline, their heads bent close together, and eventually it seemed the most natural thing in the world to see those two, hand in hand.

They were married that November—the eleventh or the twelfth, I forget now exactly which, but forty years ago, almost to the day. The wedding was at the Howells' place, with most of our neighbors there, and Caroline looked lovely in the blue muslin dress I'd made, with lace ruffles around her throat, and white satin ribbons fluttering over her curls.

All that next year, Caroline wore that blue dress to Emmaus Chapel whenever preaching was held, until her first child—that was Lydia—was coming along and the bodice got too snug. When Caroline died, we thought of burying her in that wedding dress, but it seemed too frilled for a proper shroud.

Lydia wore that same blue dress when *she* got married, because she wanted something of her mama's. I helped her make it over to fit, but then afterwards we packed it away again. In fact, it's lying still in one of these trunks up here. I reckon I could find it if I really wanted to, but it's almost dark, and I need to go downstairs to Ike again.

Chapter Six

Sunday, November 11th, 1860

The world outside has quieted down, now that it's almost dusk, but this morning seemed uncommonly loud for a Sabbath. Every church in town, I do believe, decided to hold a service the exact same day, and bells were ringing everywhere. Afterwards, I could hear folks calling to one another, and it didn't all sound like pious fellowship to me.

I wish to goodness things would settle down again, so Ike could die in peace. All week it's been like this, with people seizing the least excuse to gather in the streets and speculate where events will lead. *South Carolina...South Carolina...* rolls from nearly every tongue, and anywhere you turn, there's someone who has a second cousin living down to Charleston or Columbia, or who's just received a letter from there. Of course, I haven't been talking politics myself, with so much else on my mind.

This evening, I'm extra desirous of silence and the chance to sit alone for a while, because the house has been full of company all day long. Lydia's family drove into town this morning, and two of Ike's boys, Dan and Essau, came by the house after dinner and stayed until just a while ago. Essau's wife and baby were with them too, so that we had to rustle chairs from one room to the other, just to have a place for everyone to sit. With all the commotion, Ike seemed to rally, at least enough to recognize the boys, but a few minutes more, and he slipped back into his torpor.

After awhile, the boys got bored with Sabbath talk, and they launched into a lively exchange about South Carolina's doings and what this election means—with their dying daddy asleep right there. Essau keeps store in Kinston, and it's not often that he has a chance to visit this way, so I let them be, sickroom or not. To my knowledge, neither one of those boys has ever set foot in South Carolina, and I marvel at how they can be so certain what South Carolina will do, and what will transpire on account of it.

Part of me found it annoying to have them carrying on, because I do not want to hear that the world is a tinder-box, just waiting for a spark. Such talk makes me more unsettled than I already am. Don't *I*, of all people, know how quickly flames can spread? And yet I do confess, I found the boys' conversation a respite of a sort. I am tired of thinking about nothing but chamber pots and my own personal woe.

It was a wholesome distraction as well to have Lydia's family around the house today. Jesse, her husband, sat in the kitchen and watched as Lina helped her mama roast the chickens they'd brought. It's times like today that I acknowledge what a strain it must be for Lydia to keep staying in town with me, and yet I need her so. It's a lonesome task to nurse a dying man, night and day. It helps to have someone spell you a while, so you can fill your lungs with unpolluted air and stretch the kinks from your bones.

I like Lydia immensely. And I always have, right from the first, when she was only a curly-haired babe bouncing on Caroline's lap. Lydia has grown up to be one of the kindest women I know, and I feel bad, taking her away from Jesse, the children, and the farm. At least it's November, and the crops are in.

And, thankfully, Lina is old enough to take over things in her mama's absence—she's about the age I was when my own mama died. Lydia says that Lina knows her way around a kitchen, and I could see that today. Lina's short and pretty, like her mama used to be—and like Caroline. I can see the resemblance clear as anything. And it seems I'm not the only one who's noticed how the girl has flowered. They were teasing her today about one of the neighborhood lads, who lives down the road a piece, and Lina, of course, was blushing and denying all the way. Lord, don't I remember? It doesn't seem all that long ago since I was watching her mama carry on the exact same way.

Ah, the romance of youth! I have always wondered: Is it a regular cycle that Nature puts everyone through? I mean, is it simply a case of looking down one day and noticing that you've put forth blooms, and then searching for the nearest apple tree, in order to pollinate, and thus to bear your proper fruit? Has Nature, from the beginning, decreed that every apple tree shall behave the exact same way?

But some folks say courting is a practical matter and has nothing at all to do with blossoms in the spring, or even eating apples. It's just that women weren't meant to hammer and plow, and men weren't made to cook, so pairing up is the most convenient way of arranging things. I know there's folks who say that's how it was with Isaac Howell and me—and I don't deny it wasn't a part. But only a part.

Then again, other folks have such faith in the Lord Almighty that they claim every marriage performed on this earth has been specifically arranged by the Lord—and they claim the same for every birth, and every departure too.

Personally, I don't hold the Lord accountable for what's happening to Isaac now, and I have to confess my doubts that the Lord Almighty troubles Himself to pick out one particular man for every living woman. He may have sent them in pairs, male and female, into Noah's ark, but that was ages ago, and it doesn't necessarily mean He operates the same today. I simply cannot imagine the Lord Almighty sitting down every morning to pick out brides and grooms, not as many folks as live in the world these days.

Of course, I *did* believe that once—but I don't any more. You can call me ungrateful, if you will, but I abandoned that notion a considerable while ago, although up to the age of twenty-one, I did assume that the Lord in His eternal wisdom would provide a husband for me. I too would have a hearth, where I would rock my own blood child. I clung to that notion, and took it for granted, despite everything. Hadn't Ike married Caroline? And wasn't my brother James courting Rose-Ellen Howell?

I could find no fault with Rose-Ellen. In fact, I deemed her one of my closest friends—both Caroline and I felt that way. Rose-Ellen was fair-haired and pleasant. She was quiet and competent, and I thought she'd make James a perfect wife. I told him so more than once, and indeed it proved to be the case. I wasn't even surprised when he told me his intentions, because marrying Rose-Ellen Howell seemed such a natural thing for my brother James to do.

It's just that there wasn't another Howell left for *me*. There was no one for me, and as time went on, it grew all the more apparent. I was twenty-two years old when James brought Rose-Ellen home to live. I was older than either Caroline or Rose-Ellen, and yet I'd never been courted. Oh, of course I'd been flirted with, and I'd had my share of flattery from neighborhood men who'd say, "How d'ye do, Miss Dorcas, and ain't you looking right smart today!"

I've never spurned compliments, but neither do I let them spin my head. I wasn't what you'd call unsightly. I had all my teeth, and my hair was just as dark and curly as Caroline's. But I was twenty-two years old, and five-feet-eight-inches tall, and there simply weren't enough apple trees to go around. It was clear that the Lord was tending to other business instead of finding a husband for me.

And yet there were certain compensations. I had my painting, my sewing, and my pride. I had good health and the vigor of youth. I enjoyed the warm comfort of family and friends. First Caroline and Ike, and then James and Rose-Ellen assured me that I'd always have a home with them and would never be a burden or intrusion. The choice was mine, so I cast my lot with James and Rose-Ellen. All things considered, that seemed the wisest thing to do.

But then at supper one night, some few weeks after his marriage, James informed us that he was considering a move to Fayetteville. He was thinking, he said, of giving up the mail-riding and moving down there for good. He was tired of trying to keep up with the horses and the farm, while spending so much time away from home. He was married now and wanted to settle down. Besides, he hankered to go into business for himself, and in fact had begun making inquiries along that line. He'd thought about a livery stable, on account of the horses. Or maybe he could run a store, like Ike and his daddy did. What did Rose-Ellen think?

Well, Rose-Ellen didn't know what to say, not at first she didn't, and I myself was so startled that I misswallowed the hoecake I was chewing. I choked and sputtered so that James had to whack me hard across the shoulders, and we got distracted for a while, until James drew our attention back to the matter at hand.

"Fayetteville?" Rose-Ellen said. "Why, I'd miss Mama such a heap, and Belle too—but I reckon that's an adjustment I'm willing to make."

Rose-Ellen had the advantage of me. She had been to Fayetteville once, about five years before, and had brought me and Caroline each a length of velvet ribbon—her daddy's store never carried such fancy things.

I sat in silence while James and Rose-Ellen discussed this new idea. I was fearful, you see, that James' wonderful plans didn't have space for me. The more James and Rose-Ellen talked, the more I conjured up in my mind a town that had regular laid-out streets and shops that sold all manner of goods, that had steamboats docking at the pier and scores of travelers passing through. When you've never been any place at all, have never even set foot in a town of more than a hundred folks, when you have always had to rely on partial information delivered second-hand, then a town like Fayetteville seems like the golden answer to all your dreams. I sat at the supper table with my visions of Fayetteville shimmering before me, so real I could practically hear the coaches rattling through the streets—and yet it was still, for me, entirely out of reach. I was so entranced with my visions that it took me a moment to realize that James was speaking directly to me.

"Dorcas, you've been sitting there mighty quiet—and that's not like you. I thought for sure you'd shout with joy, the very first mention of Fayetteville. In fact, I was worried that you'd hop right up from this table and start packing your things, before we'd even agreed what we want to do."

"You mean it, James? You intend to take *me* along, and you're not just saying that? Because I reckon it's not too late for me to move in with Ike and Caroline."

"My beloved sister," James declared, "I am *counting* on you being there—and will be mad as all get-out if you're not."

Well, I did whoop for joy then, and cry and carry on, and my excitement continued all through the next few weeks while we laid our plans. We knew we were moving for sure, but we had to figure out what we'd be moving to.

Our fate was determined when one of Fayetteville's hotel-keepers decided to sell out and move to his daughter's plantation. He was getting old, and his wife had died the year before, and I suppose he was tired of hustling to meet the wants of traveling folks. It was the same lodging place where James had stayed for the past five years, so this man knew of James' intentions and offered him first chance to buy the place.

We sat up half one night, James and Rose-Ellen and me, working out what we would do. The old man's price was steep. The Golden Sun was several blocks away from State House Square, James said, and had grown rather old and shabby. Still, it was already known to a great many traveling men, and Fayetteville was a growing town.

One of our tasks that evening, as I remember, was to count all the coins that James had saved over the years. His jug was so heavy it slipped from his hands and broke into smithereens, but we were mighty excited that evening and did not even care. We just laughed to see it shatter. The coins rolled every which way, and we had to get on our hands and knees to gather them up. In fact, next morning James crawled beneath the house, like a chicken or a dog, to pick up those that had fallen between the cracks of the floor.

Well, anyway, James and Rose-Ellen and me counted those coins and made the tally. And when we were done, I went and got *my* jug and brought it to the table too, and dumped my coins into a pile. At first James wouldn't hear of it.

"Now, Dorcas, you go and put this jug right back on the mantelpiece where it belongs. What kind of brother do you think I am, to use *your* money for *my* establishment? It may be close, but I expect I can manage, between selling off the horses and this place too."

I can be stubborn, and James knew it. We always understood each other, eye to eye. It's because we both were cut from the same length of cloth. I was close to Caroline, especially in womanly matters, but with James I could talk and argue about so many other things.

"James," I said, "I will *not* move to Fayetteville unless you invest my money the same as yours. I'll stay right here and rot unless you agree to let me do my full and rightful share."

So I convinced him, and truth is, I think James was relieved, because buying the Golden Sun was a costly venture.

But it wasn't pure generosity on my part. I have always held the belief that anything truly good must be paid for in some way, else it's liable to prove out harmful in the end. I *wanted* to sacrifice for this dream called Fayetteville. I wanted to earn the right of going there, so that Fayetteville would never turn sour but would always live up to those happy notions buzzing through my head.

Chapter Seven

Monday, November 12th, 1860

I always count it a blessing when Monday turns out clear, like today, and I can get my clothes-washing done while the week's still new. Sometimes I wish I could stretch my entire life out to dry in the sun, so that everything could be fresh and bright again. But these days even the bedsheets don't come clean, what with all our sickroom stains.

Some days I set my ironing table beside Ike's bed, and I talk to him just as if he were awake enough to hear. I try not to let the washing fall too far behind. It is one of my fears that Ike will have an accident, and there won't be enough clean linen at hand to take care of things. That almost happened the other day. You'd think that a household endowed with eighteen bedsheets would never run out, but Ike had such a spell one afternoon that I went through my entire supply. I prayed there'd be time enough for the laundry to dry, before I had to change his bed again.

I sent to Ike's store this morning for a bolt of muslin, so I can stitch up another two or three sheets, just in case. All this, just when I thought that my sheet-making days were surely through.

Stitching bedsheets always puts me in mind of the first few weeks I spent in Fayetteville. It was early October when we moved, harvest time, and folks had brought in their crops to sell. They came from everywhere, and as we passed through the outskirts of town, we could see them camped by their wagons, cooking supper over their fires. I had never seen anything like it, but James seemed scarcely to notice. We passed a cluster of houses, lined up close against the road, their elbows almost touching, and then James turned a corner and drew the horses to a halt.

There she stood: our *Golden Sun*. I wasn't prepared, even after all James' talk, for the sight of a big frame house, two stories tall and painted yellow, with twin verandahs across the front. I wasn't prepared, either, for the sight of several gentlemen sitting on those verandahs with their feet propped on the rail—or, as we stepped inside, for the noisy crowd waiting for their supper. James recognized a few, and called the men by name, while Rose-Ellen and I stood meekly by.

I was hungry and cold, nervous and excited—and dreadfully aware of how grimy we appeared. I wanted to bathe my face and eat a hot meal, and then to run back outside and explore every street of that amazing town. But, as I learned the minute we stepped through that front door, innkeepers must take no personal thought of food or comfort until their guests have all been satisfied.

Mr. Jonah McDougan, the man who'd sold James the place, was supposed to remain at hand for our first day or two, but instead he'd packed up and departed the noon before. Perhaps he had good reason, I don't know. Or perhaps James had simply misunderstood. There had been some misunderstanding as well about which furnishings went along with the place itself, because when we arrived, there weren't enough bedsheets for all the guests, and three of the beds lacked coverlets. First thing, in fact, I had to unpack my would-be wedding quilts to serve as cover for our paying guests, else there'd have been an altercation for sure, to mark our arrival at Fayetteville.

I cannot begin to describe the confusion that reigned our first evening, and indeed for the entire next week or so. All the beds had been taken, and there was no place left for James and Rose-Ellen and me, so we made up pallets and slept on the parlor floor. It was almost midnight before we were settled. Even then, tired as I was, I could not immediately sleep. The difference was too startling. I was accustomed to a quiet country cabin. The only sounds I was used to were the natural ones of crickets and frogs, and maybe a horse's neigh from our own barnyard, or an owl's screech from the woods beyond. But now, suddenly, I found myself in a thin-walled house that was filled with close to two dozen strangers, all men. And the sounds of town, even at darkest midnight, are different from those of woods and farm. Occasionally I'd catch a drift of drunken laughter, and then the patrol tramping by to round up any Negroes who'd slipped past curfew. The town clock tolled each hour, and I was not used to keeping such a particular count of time's passing.

The missing bedsheets and coverlets may not have been carried away by Mr. McDougan, though we never knew, one way or the other. With the Golden Sun left overnight only in the charge of servants—and unproved servants at that—we were lucky to have any bedsheets at all, much less glassware and spoons. I'm surprised that more of our guests didn't help themselves.

Mr. McDougan had personally owned the servants that the Golden Sun required—a cook, an ostler, and one or two others to fetch and sweep. He had offered to sell James his Negroes along with the place—for a considerable sum, of course—and had tried to make James believe that buying those four Negroes was a charitable thing to do, else they'd likely be bought by strangers and torn away from the only home they knew. The Golden Sun's Negroes were much too spoiled, Mr. McDougan insisted, to be of use in anyone's cotton field. He doubted his daughter's husband would even be willing to take them on.

I'm not sure what Mr. McDougan did, whether he sold those Negroes or not, but I do know that James wouldn't buy them. For one thing, all our resources had been expended just in acquiring the place itself. We didn't have the funds to trade in human flesh. Besides, my brother James was opposed to slavery and always had been. That was a rare enough view in those days, but it's even rarer now. Today, in fact, I doubt an inn like ours could prosper, if word got around that the innkeeper harbored such opinions as James held to back then.

James had made arrangements for the help we needed, and the free Negro family he'd hired had been on the job two days when we ourselves appeared. Jim was a tall, quiet man who did our gardening and stablework, and his wife Delilah had charge of the kitchen. Their two oldest children, not quite grown, waited tables and such. Delilah was a stocky woman, dark as molasses, with a wide gap between her front teeth. It was clear that she knew how to cook, on the family level at least, but it took her some adjustment to figure how many victuals to fix for the crowd we daily had to feed. Sometimes she'd overshoot the mark, and the food would spoil and waste, but other nights there wouldn't be quite enough to go around, and then James and Rose-Ellen and me would sit at table with our guests and feign to have no appetite at all.

I needn't have worried about seeing the sights of Fayetteville, because the next morning after our arrival, James pressed upon me a handkerchief full of coins and sent me to town with Delilah to buy supplies. Her middle

44

son Timothy went along with us too, pushing a barrow before him, to transport our purchases home.

Fayetteville's old wooden State House sat in the middle of a square, and beneath its arches was spread the most fascinating array of fixings I'd ever seen. Baskets of cornmeal and rice. Piles of apples and yams. Salt fish, sausage links, and frightened hens. I was overwhelmed by the sight of so much abundance, but Delilah pushed her way through the crowd, pinching, weighing, and sorting.

"Here, grab a-hold to this one!" she'd say, thumping a pumpkin or a squash for Timothy to tote to his barrow.

I concluded each transaction with the coins required but was not prepared for how quickly those coins could disappear. The earnings from a whole day's sewing, gone in a flash! And when we were done at the market, we proceeded to a shop for coffee beans and lemons, raisins and cloves. Items that had been the rarest luxuries back to home were taken for granted here.

By midafternoon, in fact, I had been inside some half dozen shops and bought two bolts of muslin and eight yards of plain white linen, because many of our napkins had disappeared as well. And by bedtime that second night, I had already finished hemming my first bedsheet and started on a second one.

I set myself a steady task. Every morning those first few weeks, as soon as the marketing was done, I'd find myself a quiet corner and work straight through, as long as the light held good. Two sheets a day, and three napkins, and a pair of pillow shams. It was boring work, I do admit, with straight seams and no color—not like the fancy silks I'd grown accustomed to. Indeed, it was a good while before I was free to sew for hire again, because I had so many necessities to make. Window curtains, dish towels, and the like. Even now, I cannot think of our move to

Fayetteville without feeling a certain tightness in my spine, from hunching so steadily over my work.

Gradually, though, James and Rose-Ellen and me began to get things sorted out. Each of us had our duties to attend to, except that Rose-Ellen often felt poorly those first few weeks. James and me were worried for a while, until it grew evident what condition was causing her to feel so indisposed.

Business was good, although occasionally we hit a slow spell. There were three other hotels in town, larger ones, which attracted most of the trade. The stages all departed from the Lafayette, which was closer to the State House, although most of the drivers stayed with us, for the sake of economy. We were not a fancy place, and the crowd we served was mostly basic folks. Sometimes, in fact, they were rowdier than we could wish, and James had to exercise considerable tact and restraint. Of course, Rose-Ellen and me always disappeared upstairs as soon as supper was done. In those early days, the Golden Sun served only men, except for occasional evenings when our parlor and dining room had been let for a private supper, in which case we'd have the pleasure of welcoming ladies too.

Our purchase, as James had warned, was thriving, but it badly needed attention and repairs. First thing, James decided that we ought to replace the warped and faded sign that hung from the front verandah, and he asked me would I mind to paint one up. Would I mind, indeed! I was delighted to have an excuse to set those bedsheets aside and reach for my watercolors instead. I must have sketched a dozen ideas before I settled upon the final scheme: a blazing golden sun against a bright blue sky, with just a trace of rolling green land beneath.

James fixed me up a board, four feet long and eighteen inches high, and went with me to buy the paint I'd need. I used powdered gilt to give the sun a golden sheen, and the letters I made bright red. It was a huge, bold sign, and painting it gave me immense satisfaction.

When I look back now upon those first few weeks in Fayetteville, a hundred memories press in close, all at once: sewing bedsheets, painting that sign, going to market, and walking through the streets with James. It was such a lively place, with so much to see and do, that I never tired of running errands.

But it wasn't all perfect happiness down to Fayetteville, and sometimes I have to remind myself of that—lest I be tempted to escape these present woes by dwelling on the past. There was ugliness in Fayetteville too, amidst all the wonders, and sometimes you'd happen upon it when you least expected.

I remember one bright morning, during those early weeks, when I went with James towards the courthouse, for some reason that I don't recall. We passed an open doorway, and it was clear from the sound of things that a sale was under way. Immediately, before James could halt me, I stepped inside, thinking that someone had died and their goods were being disposed of. I thought we might purchase some extra dishes or chairs—when you're running an inn, you always look out for such things.

But as soon as I stepped into that room, I saw my mistake. On a long bench behind the auctioneer sat maybe a dozen Negroes, two of them mere toddling children, and one a frail old woman, stooped with age. And on the block, in front of everyone, stood a young woman about the age of seventeen, tall and plump. Beneath her homespun dress she wore several petticoats, some of them plain and some of calico. There were gentlemen swarming around her like flies to honey, and one of them had the audacity to poke his finger into her mouth and feel that woman's teeth, as though he were judging a horse, and another one reached right under her petticoats and squeezed the muscles of her leg—if she had been a mule, she'd have kicked him flat. That was all I saw, because my brother James hauled me straight back out of there.

"Dorcas, don't you have a grain of sense? Can't you tell where you don't belong?"

He spoke with gritted teeth, and yet I knew he was riled not at me but at what we both had seen. We proceeded on down the street, and the entire time I lived at Fayetteville I never stepped foot in that place again, and never again witnessed such a sale. Sometimes, though, when I accompanied James to the wharf, I couldn't help but see a gang of Negroes chained together, being led from the steamship decks, on their way to somebody's turpentine plantation or somebody's cotton field. And today, when I think of Fayetteville, I have to remember those things too.

It's not that I wasn't used to the sight of Negroes. Didn't Belle Yancey own Negroes? Didn't some of the other farmers I knew, up here to home? But somehow it wasn't entirely the same: seeing a Negro at work in someone's field or a kitchen is not the same as seeing an entire group in chains. There's no avoiding the ugliness then.

Chapter Eight

Tuesday, November 13th, 1860

Sometimes as I sit beside Ike's bed, I study his face for clues of the Isaac Howell that used to be. But he lies now so pale and still, his eyelids closed, his breath rasping in and out between parted lips, that it is hard for me to find much trace of the strength that used to come from this man I love.

I wish now that I'd painted Isaac's likeness some thirty years ago, when he was in his manly prime, but I reckon it never occurred to me back then. Besides, I doubt it would have been proper, to sit alone with Isaac Howell and paint his portrait, on account of him belonging to Caroline. And then, once we were married, Ike and me, I kept so occupied with the children and the household that I never thought I should spare the time to do my husband's portrait.

It was on account of my brother James that I took up likeness painting, during my first year at Fayetteville. James was always suggesting that I paint one thing or another. After the success of my sign, he asked me to choose new colors for the parlor—I picked a cheerful blue-green, with ivory woodwork and just a touch of russet here and there. And then on the fireplace board I painted a woods-and-river scene, which was quite the style back then. I made it autumn, with red and gold trees above the dark brown water. When the scene was done, it evoked considerable comment from the gentlemen who stayed at the Golden Sun, and that pleased my brother James.

We were trying to elevate the Golden Sun and give the place a slightly higher tone. We knew we could never compete with the Lafayette, but we wanted to establish a reputation for pleasant quarters and wholesome food. Delilah had charge of the kitchen and did a most creditable job. Certainly I myself had never been used to such fine victuals, though there *are* folks who expect fancy confections every day. Plain cake is not enough, but what it has to have tinted icing too.

James was the one who greeted our guests, kept track of the money, and performed the largest portion of the repairs we undertook. My main task was to see that our surroundings were as comfortable as we could make them—to decide that we needed a blue-striped curtain here or a vase of posies there.

For the parlor I did that river scene, and then for the dining room I painted several arrangements of flowers and fruit. In fact, when I went to market with Delilah, I would keep my eyes open for something colorful to use as a still life. One of those paintings, I remember, was of some beautiful pale green grapes spilling over the edge of a copper bowl. For another, I set a pineapple among some lemons and added a few red lilies. Delilah, I also remember, made a pineapple cake and two lemon pies after that particular painting was through.

But painting landscapes and fruit is one thing, and doing the likeness of a real live human being is another matter entirely. I might never have worked my way into the portrait business had not James insisted that he wanted a picture of Rose-Ellen holding their newborn baby on her lap. That must have been about July, when we'd been at Fayetteville not quite a year, because my nephew Jeremy was born in early June. He was still just a mewling tike when James asked me to record in paint the happiest, proudest event of his life. I doubt Rose-Ellen could have done anything that pleased my brother more than bearing him a son, and Jeremy grew up to prove worthy of his daddy's esteem. The tragedy is that Rose-Ellen never bore but one more living child, and that boy drowned at the age of seventeen.

It was hot as blazes that summer. Perhaps it was really no hotter than any other summer at Fayetteville, but trying to appease an infant long enough to paint his likeness can make you dreadfully aware of the heat, not to mention all the insects flying by. Every morning for a fortnight, Rose-Ellen put on her Sunday frock and her best lace-edged cap, and she dressed the baby in the christening frock I'd made, and then I posed them in the parlor. I was perhaps foolish to attempt my very first portrait in oils, which are far more tedious than watercolors can ever be, but I thought that a painting done in oils would be more likely to last through the years. Hadn't James said that in his dotage he wanted to see his beautiful wife and oldest son just as they looked right then? Besides, I was trying to expand my skills.

When you paint rivers, or even those simple Bible scenes I used to do, then you're free to arrange your picture any way you choose, and you can use whichever colors you feel like on that day. But when you attempt to paint the likeness of another human being, then responsibility rests heavy upon you—or at least that's how it always seemed to me. You want to come up with a reasonable likeness, so that anyone who sees your picture will say, yes, that *is* Miss So-and-So. People have different distinctions, and different moods. For some folks, what you're trying to catch is the tilt of their head, or a particular expression that hovers about the eyes, but then with another person the essential feature may be something else entirely.

Every person I've painted, I've always tried to show that person at their best. There's so much ugliness and trouble in this world, it seems to me, that I make an extra effort to discern something good about whoever sits there posing. With some folks, that comes easy—while for others, I admit, finding the good requires a considerable search.

Rose-Ellen's virtues were clearly evident, of course, though with that first portrait I had great difficulty catching her uniqueness. In the end, I produced a tolerable picture of a pretty young matron with a baby, but I couldn't help but feel that the Rose-Ellen of the picture was much too stiff and solemn, not the graceful person I knew her to be. Over the years I had several opportunities to paint Rose-Ellen's portrait, and eventually I produced one that satisfied even me, but that first likeness was the one that always pleased my brother most.

By the time my nephew Jeremy was born, we were pretty much settled into our life at the Golden Sun. By then, we were caught up on repairs, and I was through making all those bedsheets. In fact, I had begun sewing for hire again, at least in a modest way. At Fayetteville, as I quickly learned, there were several seamstresses and milliners already established, and I could no longer lay claim to being the smartest needle around. On the other hand, at Fayetteville there were far more ladies needing attention, and much more scrutiny of the fashion plates from New York and Paris. We may not have been a large metropolis, but we *were* a fair-sized market town, with regular travelers passing through, and we weren't so rustic but what we didn't try to catch wind of the newest styles to emulate.

At first I had to prove myself by stitching basic things that offered little challenge—table linen and plain white hollander shirts. Who would trust an unknown woman with expensive silk? But I was glad enough to be collecting coins again. Much of what I earned went for something needed about the place—vinegar cruets or candlesticks—but it wasn't long before I had a small fund for buying canvas and paint.

After my first attempt at painting Rose-Ellen, I set about doing portraits whenever I had the chance. My nephew Jeremy was painted at regular intervals—I doubt there's many children whose infancy was recorded in such detail. I painted my brother James standing at the door of the Golden Sun. I even painted Delilah, standing amidst her pots and pans, with her two oldest children on either side. Gradually I grew more skillful at judging what proportions the human face requires, and I began to develop techniques for painting frocks and such.

If my brother James had been more modest, I might never have worked my way into doing portraits, beyond my own household. But James, bless his soul, hung that first picture of Rose-Ellen in the front hall of the Golden Sun, where anyone could see, and when his own portrait was done, he hung that too. As a consequence of those two pictures hanging in our hall, various people about town began to inquire after my services.

I don't pretend I was ever the equal of those portrait-painters who ply the trade for real, such as my dear Yankee friend, who passed through town and stayed with us for such a while. I know I never came close to the talents *he* had. But not everyone could afford the services of a professional limner, nor did they always choose to wait for a traveling painter to happen through town again.

With such constant risk of death's snatching a loved one away, many folks would decide to have a clumsy portrait done, rather than no painting at all. Back then, of course, there was no such thing as the daguerreotype, or the camera either, so paint and brush were the only practical way of recording someone's likeness.

Gradually, word spread through Fayetteville that Miss Dorcas Reed was adept at painting likenesses, so every now and again someone would ask me to paint their children's portrait. Other times, a just-wed man and his wife would want their likenesses done. At first, I was delighted simply to have the opportunity to try my hand, though I did accept donations towards the cost of paint. Soon, however, the requests came so frequently that likeness-painting began to interfere with my sewing for hire, and I had to make a choice. I determined that I would paint for three or four hours every afternoon, and the rest of the time would tend to my sewing. I did one or two paintings a month, but not all of them were likenesses. Some folks wanted their fireplaces painted with a scene, or maybe they'd taken a fancy to one of the fruit arrangements I'd done for our dining room.

It still seems a miracle, when I think about it now, but I actually developed a regular painting trade. That's not to say that I did all the painting that was required in Fayetteville—far from it. I never attempted outdoor signs, beyond the one I did for the Golden Sun, though personally I would have enjoyed that. I never painted carriage doors, nor climbed a ladder to stencil a wall, except for my own attic chamber and one or two other rooms at the Golden Sun. Naturally, being a lady, there were limits to what I could undertake.

I cannot express sufficiently the joy and satisfaction I found in those years of painting. I was never bored. Each portrait, each scene, presented challenge anew. Just the act of painting was its own reward, but it's an extra blessing when other people appreciate the work you've labored to produce.

Even my needlework began to be affected by the painting I did. Before long, the ladies of town were hiring my services not for plain white shirts, nor even for party frocks, but for fancy quilt squares or fine embroidery work. Back then, we didn't have available the ready-stamped patterns that folks are so fond of today, and often I would be asked to devise a floral border or a special center square. Sometimes I'd be hired to do the stitching myself, and other times the lady in question would perform the needlework.

Fayetteville. Those dozen years now seem to me an entire patchwork of color, rich with the oils of my palette and with bright embroidery silks. I was not married—and kept ever mindful of that—but I *was* richly blessed, far more than I deserved, with work that I truly loved.

Occasionally, even back then, I would ask myself whether my painting had any true value, judged in a moral way. I knew, of course, what my Quaker forebears would say—my Grandmother Lacey, for instance, long since deceased but still remembered in her plain homespun frock. Hadn't I set aside useful pursuits for the sake of making images? And wasn't I guilty of flattering folks, of encouraging their vanity and sin? I asked my brother James about it once, but he advised me to put such musings out of mind.

"Dorcas," he said, "surely there's no harm in taking the likeness of God's own creatures, as long as you acknowledge the partiality of what you've done and don't mistake it for true creation itself. And if it's *moral* you want to talk, then surely there's weightier notions to worry yourself about—why, just look around you."

So I laid my qualms aside and kept on painting. I must have done more than a hundred likenesses during my years at Fayetteville. I painted scores of children, dressed in their Sunday best. I painted strangers and friends. I painted

James and Rose-Ellen and Caroline, and almost all of my nieces and nephews.

But never once, not in all those years, did I paint the likeness of Isaac Howell. And now, *I* am the one who yearns for some record, however partial, of my dear husband's face. Something tangible to remember him by.

Chapter Nine

Wednesday, November 14th, 1860

This morning Ike roused up and actually talked to me for an hour or so. He wanted to know what all the noise was about outside. This was Muster Day, and most of the able-bodied men in town were marching around the court-house—you could hear the drums from here. You'd have thought it was Independence Day, from the sound of things. In fact, they came right down this street and across the creek bridge to the outskirts of town, where they commenced firing volleys. This didn't appear to be just an ordinary muster, because half the town was following along and hollering them on, and the Light Infantry staged a review, with fancy stepping and such.

When they came tramping by, Ike sent me out to the front verandah so I could give a first-hand report. He wanted to know what it was all about but then seemed confused when I tried to explain about Abraham Lincoln and what that may foretell. Ike used to be sharp about politics, and I was loathe to point out how much has lately passed him by.

57

I think it was the notion of soldiering that somehow stirred his blood and made Ike's mind run clear—some instinctive answer to the call of the marching drum. Ike always enjoyed Muster Day. He liked tramping around with the other men, shooting guns and such. He kept up mustering, in fact, several years beyond when he might legally have ceased. And then, when he did give it up, he would spend Muster Day on the porch of the store, calling out encouragement.

Ike was never called upon to fight an actual skirmish, like those men marching today stand a good chance to do, if all this talk keeps up. Once, though, he had to go with several others out past Stony Creek, where some poor farmer was holed up in his neighbor's cabin, pointing a shotgun straight at that neighbor's wife, and with several little children in the cabin too. It was a dispute over boundaries, and that man had gone plumb crazy. He'd already shot all his neighbor's pigs and even a mule, and the bleeding carcasses lay scattered over the yard by the time Ike and the others got there. They finally coaxed that man outside by setting a jug of spirits against the cabin door. But next morning, in jail, that poor man was found to have hung himself.

Still, I doubt that incident, tragic though it was, compares to the experience of all-out war. I don't really know, because I myself have been spared from any direct encounter with war. Of course there was that British business when I was twelve, but that was the summer my sister Nancy died, and my grief was all for her. What did I care about someone fighting off to sea, or up to Washington City?

But the men who marched by here today have their minds on war—you could tell by watching them, by all the extra hullabaloo. Some folks claim war is inevitable. Mose Griffin, who helps at Ike's store, says there's already a run on calico and coffee, on things that come by sea or from up North somewhere. It seems that folks are getting ready for a siege. But when *I* consider such matters, I side with those who say that South Carolina can't determine what *we* ought to do. Myself, I hold with those who aren't yet ready to leap to such extreme.

Either way, though, folks say that we ought to make plans for seizing the federal arsenal, down to Fayetteville, just as sound precaution. They say if it *does* come to war, we'll want to keep those guns from Yankee hands.

That arsenal was not even built when I was living at Fayetteville, but I do remember Muster Days, when everyone gathered in Courthouse Square. And I remember the Light Infantry and how they used to strut and rat-a-tat behind the Presbyterian Church.

And, as long as I live, I shall never forget the grand procession the morning when the Marquis de Lafayette—*General* Lafayette—arrived at Fayetteville. Such drum-beating and flag-waving I had never seen, and indeed have witnessed nothing to surpass it, to this day. Even the pouring rain could not dampen our spirits, though it ruined the bunting on the State House and maybe shortened the orations a bit. Standing in that crowd was one time I was glad to be uncommonly tall, so that I could catch a glimpse of General Lafayette with the governor by his side. Indeed, I had never seen so many notables, and even my brother James could name but half of them.

"We are plain republicans," I heard Judge Toomer proclaim. "We greet you not with pomp and gilt, but with all the fervor of our simple, honest hearts."

Simple hearts indeed! Had we gilt enough, every roof in town would have been gold that day.

I did not go to the fancy ball that night. We Methodists did not hold with dancing, and besides, at the Golden Sun we were more than busy. Folks had come from miles away. Even my attic room had been let, and I'd moved in with

James and Rose-Ellen. I did not go to the ball, but as I scurried around that evening, I did take satisfaction in knowing that several gowns, stitched in silk, were there to represent me in a way.

My moment of modest glory came the following day, at a reception the mayor gave to honor our visitor. A local notion held that our wooden State House was a perfect replica of the market house in the French town were Lafayette was born. I don't know how that notion arose, and whether it were true or merely an outflowering of our Fayetteville pride. But I do know that upstairs in that same State House, some forty years before, our North Carolina fathers had assented to the Constitution that binds together these United States.

Anyway, a few weeks before Lafayette's arrival, an idea developed that a painting of our State House would make a good memento for our guest—and I was asked to produce this scene. I wound up painting a simple picture, though it cost much effort and work, all the same. I wanted the scene to have dignity, yet I also wanted to give this honored man something true to remember us by. I sketched and painted, and discarded one version after another, until I came up with a picture that I deemed presentable.

I placed the scene in early morning, with the clock hands showing nine and sunshine slanting upon the cupola and the wood-shingled roof. At each second-story window I placed a gentleman leaning out, dressed in old-timey clothes. One was waving a flag, and one held the scales of justice, and the third held a stack of books, but whether law books or scripture, I did not indicate. And then, beneath the ground-floor arcade I painted such a market as I remembered from my first morning at Fayetteville: farmers with their hams and sacks of meal, housewives with baskets over their arms, and dozens of Negroes and children amidst the piles of plenty. I used every color in the rainbow in that market scene. When my work was done, some folks said it was splendid, but others complained that I oughtn't to have included any Negroes, not for an honored man like Lafayette. But by then it was too late to come up with something else.

On account of those complaints, I felt much trepidation at the mayor's reception and was almost afraid to watch as the mayor presented our gift to General Lafayette. I kept to the back of the room while Lafayette unfolded the wrappings. I was truly relieved when he smiled and nodded as he held the painting up.

"This is most lovely!" he exclaimed, in a voice that held the flavor of France. "I shall greatly treasure this remembrance of your kind hospitality."

I was startled then to hear the mayor call my name. My brother James nudged me forward, and I, plain Dorcas Reed, was actually introduced to the esteemed Marquis de Lafayette. He stood even taller than me and was older than I expected. His eyes were blue and direct, his forehead high—I tried to notice each detail as though I were taking his likeness, but as I studied his face he suddenly took my hand and raised it to his lips. And kissed it! He kissed my hand and spoke more words of politeness, and then I was led aside to make way for someone else.

Every important person in town was crowded into that reception room. We were all caught up together in the splendor of the occasion, sharing our admiration of that great man. Many noble words were spoken in eulogy.

And then suddenly there was a murmuring at the door, and into our midst came poor old Isham Blake, grizzled and stooped, escorted on either side by four Light Infantrymen, wearing their uniforms. Old Isham was scrubbed and neatened, but his greatcoat had obviously seen several decades of wear. Folks drew back to form a clearing as

Isham Blake passed straight through to Lafayette, who graciously hid his puzzlement.

"Begging your leave, sir," Old Isham said, bowing low.

From a pocket of his greatcoat he pulled a wooden fife and raised it to his lips, and there issued forth a stirring air, a marching tune with sharp clear notes that pierced our souls and would have had us tapping in accompaniment, except that Isham broke off midway and commenced to cough and wheeze. At that, to our astonishment, General Lafayette stepped forward and embraced old Isham Blake, clasped him tight.

"Isham!" Lafayette exclaimed. "Isham Blake! I am grateful, my dear friend, to see you still alive!"

And then, at Lafayette's request, Isham played one tune and then another. The General stood there listening to those marching airs, his head tilted to one side, an intent expression upon his face. The tunes were sprightly, and yet as we stood there listening, as we watched our honored guest and this old fifer, I sensed a sadness beneath those lilting melodies. I looked at General Lafayette and saw, to my amazement, *tears* in his eyes, which made me lose all impulse to dance and tap. Soon, many eyes were damp within that room.

Old Isham had piped at Yorktown. When Isham grew short of breath and laid his fife aside, Lafayette, our honored guest, insisted that Isham be given the softest chair and the first glass of punch.

I doubt it not when folks speak of music that can raise the dead, or of that magic piper who emptied out a town, because I myself witnessed the power of a simple tune that day at Fayetteville. And it must have been some such power that roused my husband today. The cadence of a drum drew him back from the world of sleep—at least for a while. I despise this talk of war, and yet I wish the drums would roll forever, if only that would bring my dear Isaac back to me.

Chapter Ten

Thursday, November 15th, 1860

Last evening Dan came by the house to sit with his father for an hour or so. He brought the *Harper's Weekly*, which has an engraving of Abraham Lincoln, soon to be President.

"Look a-there!" Dan said. "Did you ever see such pure-out *malice* upon the face of a man?"

I looked, but for the life of me could ascertain no evil in the countenance I saw. Of course, that magazine likeness was taken from the Yankee point of view, but Mr. Lincoln seemed to me an ordinary working man, not fully at ease in his Sunday dress-up clothes. His wife must not feed him well, because he's so painfully thin. And I've heard that he stands extra tall, but I doubt that's much advantage. Taken all together, he doesn't look stately enough to be President, but he doesn't look evil, either.

Still, I don't necessarily trust the Yankee artist who did that picture. Sometimes all it takes is a smudge, or a single jot of the pen, to transform entirely the person whose likeness you're taking. A highlight, or the curve of a line, can make all the difference between seeming amiable or grim.

It was Abraham Greene who taught me that, in September of my twenty-ninth year. We were sitting in the parlor of the Golden Sun. Abraham Greene had a sheet of paper tacked to his easel, and he was sketching a picture of me with a charcoal pencil. I was plumb amazed at how quick he could draw, his hand darting here and there.

"You see?" he said, showing me the partial sketch. "Do you see how that shadow defines the shape of your chin?"

I studied the shadow he pointed to, but I was mostly curious to see what overall effect Abraham Greene would produce, when taking the likeness of *me*. I saw myself in the glass each morning, my hair all loose and tumbling down my back—and then, once dressed, I'd look again, to see that my fichu was modestly pinned and that my cap was straight. But my looking glass was smoky and streaked, and besides, it's only natural to arrange yourself with a smile when peering at your own reflection. It's another matter entirely to see yourself as others do. Many times I myself have witnessed the nervousness that attends a first look at one's own likeness.

It was not mere vanity, however, that prompted my scrutiny of Abraham's drawing. I have many faults and sins, but surely pride of beauty is not among them. I wanted to know how I appeared to the world at large—but, more especially, I wanted to know how I appeared to Abraham Greene.

Thankfully he was kind, as well as quick of hand. He'd sketched me with my head tilted as though I were deep in thought, or listening intently—as indeed I was, to his instructions. The afternoon sunlight shone upon my hair and across one shoulder. With light and shadow he'd told it all.

"Yes," I replied, "I think I do see."

"Well then, here—try it yourself and do a sketch of me. Observe where the densest shadows are, and bear down hardest there. And where the shadow's soft, smudge it lightly with your thumb."

With that, he pinned up a fresh sheet of paper and turned the easel around to me. Then he leaned upon his chair, with his elbow propped across the top and his hand hanging free.

"Think of my face as composed of shapes," he said. "It's not just one flat surface, but a series of valleys and hills. And think of my hand the exact same way. Now look hard before you start to draw."

I had never worked with a charcoal stick before, so drew my first line rather tentatively. Abraham Greene was a broad-shouldered man, slightly taller than me, and his clean-shaven face was nearly round—even his cheeks were round. His short dark hair was thick with curls. I was clumsy with the charcoal and my shadows came too heavy.

"Never mind," Abraham said. "Just use the India rubber and lift some of the charcoal away."

It worked, to my amazement. With charcoal, nothing is ever permanent. A nose can be easily shortened. A cheek can be dimpled, and then undimpled again. When you're sketching a likeness, that serves to good advantage, but don't expect charcoal to last through the years. When my sketch of Abraham Greene was done, after many adjustments, I rolled it up and carried it to my attic room. I would use the blank side for practice, or at least that's what I told Abraham Greene.

In fact I kept that charcoal sketch, rolled up and tied with a ribbon, in the back of my bureau drawer. For weeks after that—indeed, for months—before I'd extinguish my candle each night, I'd unroll that drawing and gaze upon the likeness of Abraham Greene, as though he were God's own angel sent to guard me through the night. But with each unrolling, the sketch began to shift and blur, until finally there was no longer an image of Abraham Greene but one vast smudge, as though a fog had risen to hide him from my view.

Most nights, though, I did not need a charcoal sketch to call Abraham Greene to mind. He had been with us less than a week when I first realized that even after I'd left his presence, he seemed to be with me. It was a most strange sensation. Again and again, every night before I fell asleep I'd repeat to myself each fragment of conversation that Abraham Greene had spoken. And each morning when I first awoke, I'd find myself listening for the sound of his voice—from the back yard, perhaps. Abraham Greene had a rich full voice, but he spoke like he drew, with quickness. The rhythm of his speech was different from the talk of most folks I knew, because Abraham Greene was a Yankee, born in New York. He was merely a traveler in our midst. I forced myself to keep ever mindful of that.

There were times, though, after he'd departed Fayetteville again, that I could not for the life of me evoke the image of Abraham Greene. The more I'd try to remember him, the further away he seemed to be. Then I'd climb from bed and light my candle again and find the sable-haired brush he'd given me. I'd hold that brush as though I were laying paint upon a canvas, until once more I could picture *his* hand holding that same brush, just so, and could hear his voice talking about color and form. Then gradually his face would return to me, a living breathing man.

I'd wonder where Abraham was sleeping that night and how many hundreds of miles away. Was he in Baltimore? Or the City of Brotherly Love? I'd try to imagine what he might have seen that day and who he might have painted. Whenever I thought of Abraham Greene, whole vast worlds seemed open to me. I tantalized myself with thoughts of Abraham Greene. I tortured myself with thoughts of him.

It was the first of September, a Tuesday, that Abraham Greene first climbed the steps of the Golden Sun. I'd seen his gig from the dining room window, with *A. Greene, Limner* scrolled in red on the side. James was away on some errand, and Rose-Ellen was upstairs, putting the children to bed for their afternoon nap, so I myself was the one to answer Abraham's request for a room.

"Good afternoon, madam," he said in greeting. "I've been given to understand that this is a reasonable place for a traveling man to lodge. My name is Abraham Greene. I'm a painter, passing through."

He'd arrived from Norfolk, he said, and was making his way to Charleston. This was his first trip south, and he was finding the people most pleasant, though he couldn't say the same for the heat.

"Madam, I'll make you a small proposition," he said. "A business arrangement. I'd be willing to exchange you a portrait, against the cost of bed and board for a week or so."

I didn't know how to reply, since it was James who managed the business side of things. He was usually willing to barter and trade, but it seemed to me that another family portrait was one thing we did not need. Still, I didn't want to say that flat-out. I liked the looks of this Abraham Greene, and besides, my inquisitiveness had already taken hold. How well *did* he paint? And what was he doing here to Fayetteville?

About then, Abraham noticed those two paintings hanging in the hall.

"Has some other painter passed through here recently? If so, my stay will be shorter than I planned."

"No," I replied, "there hasn't been another painter through here since I don't know when. I did those two likenesses myself, which is why they aren't much account."

He looked surprised.

"Well, madam, you *do* have a knack!"

He sat his satchel down and went for a closer inspection.

"I like the colors you used," he said, "and I like the overall effect. But I *do* notice that the hands aren't finished as well as the rest, and hands always make such a difference. They tell part of the story too."

With that, he opened his satchel and produced a small sketchbook. He extended his left hand towards me, palm upwards, and flexed his fingers, open and closed.

"You notice the joints?" he said. "Notice how my fingers bend? They aren't straight as sticks, and neither are they simple curves. They *bend*—at the joints."

He proceeded to sketch a hand upon his pad, open-palmed with the fingers slightly bent. And then another hand, clasping the stem of a flower. And still another, resting upon an open book. Then he looked up with a grin.

"Well, now, madam," he said, in that joking way of his. "I have another proposition to make. If you have no use for portraits, then perhaps I can swap you some drawing lessons instead, fair even for a bed."

As it turned out, Abraham Greene stayed with us at the Golden Sun until early November. He was a splendid painter and put my poor efforts to shame. The difference was painfully apparent to me, although a few loyal friends claimed they liked my painting style the best. I expect that was because he charged considerably more for a full oil portrait than my simple fee.

At any rate, the word soon spread that we had a *real* painter in our midst. The mayor was the first to have his portrait done, and then the mayor's wife, and Mr. Duncan at the bank, and so it went. Several times during that period, Abraham Greene traveled to a plantation along the Cape Fear, but then he came back to us again.

Every morning, before breakfast, he'd be up painting, and then he'd head to someone's house for a sitting, where he'd sketch and sketch. At noon he'd come home again, and as soon as the meal was cleared, he'd set his easel in the dining room and start to work. I'd bring my sewing to the dining room, so I could watch him mix the paint and stroke it onto the canvas. He'd block the painting in, roughly at first, but as the hours passed, a face and human form would emerge, some person that I knew, and next would come the fine details—the lace upon a frock, the glinting chain of a watch. Sometimes he'd point out to me why he was doing thus-and-so in a particular way, but mostly he worked in comfortable silence, and I tried not to distract him.

I spent my days in sewing because naturally no one came begging a likeness of *me* while Abraham Greene was staying at Fayetteville. I understood, and was content to ply my needle instead—and to look and learn. I did paint my nephew Jeremy while Abraham was there, and David the baby, who was two that year. It was Abraham who suggested I do so, in order that he might better advise my work. The hands, the shadows, the use of subtle coloring—I pushed myself to meet his expectations. I even learned to speak of colors the way he did: ultramarine, ochre, and sienna, instead of plain old blue, yellow, and brown.

I encouraged my brother to avail himself of Abraham's offer to do a portrait of himself, Rose-Ellen, and the children. James, though, declined out of a stubborn loyalty to me. I was disappointed at that, because I myself wanted some reminder of Abraham's work to keep after he'd departed Fayetteville. And depart he would—I knew that from the first.

In fact, Abraham painted a portrait of *me*, working from the sketch he'd made that Sunday afternoon. It was a gentle portrait, warm and soft, and I think that James expected

Abraham to leave that painting behind when he left Fayetteville, but Abraham did not.

In the evening, Abraham would set his work aside. He didn't like to paint by candlelight, he said, because the colors never looked true. Often we'd sit together in the dining room, or in the parlor if it wasn't occupied by our gentlemen guests. Abraham liked to discuss how we lived in North Carolina, what crops were grown and such. Though he was sometimes given to sport and jest, he never appeared to laugh at our rustic ways.

And I, in turn, asked endless questions about what it was like to live up North. Abraham Greene had personally passed through places that I longed to see: Boston, Baltimore, and Washington City. The wonderful part was that he didn't just speak of an edifice or scene but would actually sketch it out so that I could see it too. That was pure-out magic, and I'm certain that James enjoyed those evenings too. James was always hankering to see the world, and I reckon that's why he wound up where he did.

Naturally, Abraham and I did not sit together alone, not in the evening. My brother or Rose-Ellen always had to sit with us too. I suppose that often proved an annoyance—for James, I mean—but I didn't consider it at the time.

Somehow I had the impression that Abraham Green was younger than me, though I never specifically inquired. My own age was an embarrassment, never even whispered aloud, lest I be viewed, at twenty-nine, as an ancient withered crone. The odd thing is that now I've reached a full three score, I am no longer loathe to admit my years. But of course I'm married now.

Abraham Greene was reared in New York City. His father was a tailor, and I suppose that's why Abraham seemed so knowledgeable of the fabrics I stitched. He spoke as easily of nankeen and serge as he did of ochre and ultramarine. I gather there'd been a falling out between father and son, and that it had something to do with Abraham's choosing to paint, instead of following his father's trade.

Abraham Green was a Yankee—there's no denying that. He had some unfamiliar ways, but I found them more intriguing than bothersome. Certainly he never lacked for politeness, or gratitude either, though I noticed some of our victuals did not appeal to him. But he never complained about it, the way some Yankees do, making a fuss about cornbread and yams. And he never went wild with drink or raced his horse through the streets of town, hollering at the top of his lungs, the way some Fayetteville men were prone to do.

That was a beautiful autumn, when Abraham Greene stayed with us at the Golden Sun. And that's when I first fancied myself an artist for real—though of course on a lower scale than my Yankee limner friend.

Chapter Eleven

Friday, November 16th, 1860

On a gray November morning, almost as gray as today, Abraham Greene departed from the Golden Sun. Sometime the previous day he'd finished the last of his portraits, and there was simply no reason for him to linger at Fayetteville any more. His canvases and paint were already packed in his gig. His horse had been shod, his shirts laundered.

Before breakfast, Delilah gave him a basket of victuals for the road, including two of her pecan pies. Delilah was partial to Abraham on account of some sketches he'd done of her children. He had, in fact, shown those drawings to me, for the sake of instruction, so I could observe how to highlight a Negro's dark skin.

As I sat at breakfast that day, my heart felt as leaden as the skies. And yet, at the same time, my senses had never been so alive. The peach preserves I spread upon my biscuit had never tasted so sweet nor shone with such translucency. I nearly wept at the perfection of that jam. Such, I thought, must be how a prisoner feels, eating his final meal before the hangman's noose.

For my brother James, however, that breakfast seemed a normal meal—but then, to my brother, Abraham Greene was merely another gentleman guest, and after his departure, someone else would come along to take his bed. For him, Abraham Greene was one of many travelers passing through.

But for *me*, Abraham Greene was special and could never be replaced. Abraham Greene was my painting teacher—the only teacher I've ever had. But even more, he was my friend. Perhaps that's why I gathered the nerve to speak out like I did.

"Mister Greene," I came right out and said, "maybe you wouldn't mind some company as far as Clarendon Bridge. I want to see how it feels, riding in a limner's gig."

Such a look, such a smile, flashed upon Abraham's face. He made his final adjustments, and I put on my bonnet and shawl. When Abraham helped me up to the seat of his gig, his hand felt warm—that was the first time I ever placed my hand in his. Then he climbed up, and away we went.

Abraham Greene, usually so quick of tongue, had little to say as we rolled through the streets of Fayetteville. I thought at first that he wished I weren't along, but when I ventured to glance at him, there was a smile upon his face, and I noticed he was holding his horse to the slowest possible walk. Instead of heading straight to Clarendon Bridge, Abraham turned south towards Mallett's Pond, where the water was dark and murky, matching the heaviness of the sky.

"Why, Mister Greene," I said, "I thought you were traveling to South Carolina! This isn't the way at all!"

"Miss Reed, I'm aware of that," Abraham said. "I'm simply taking the long way around, because I want to be able to say I've seen this town from every possible perspective."

The seat of his gig was narrow. We were wedged in cozily, despite our stiff politeness, and Abraham's shoulder kept brushing mine. I wanted to tell him how grateful I was for all he'd taught me. I wanted to say that my painting would never be the same. I started to speak but emitted only a sigh.

"Miss Reed," Abraham finally said, "have you ever been to South Carolina?"

"No," I answered. "I've never been anywhere, except home and here—and I thank the Lord that I made it to *here.*"

Had Abraham been some other man, he might have taken advantage of my innocence. He might have put his arms around me and stolen a kiss. And had I been some other woman, a younger one perhaps, I might have headed off with him to South Carolina, leaving my own good name behind. I thought of doing so as we rolled slowly along. And countless times, after that day, I wished that we *had* been bold and impulsive, instead of so concerned about doing the right and proper thing.

Eventually we reached Clarendon Bridge, and Mister Otis Campbell hobbled over to collect the toll.

"Will that be one or two?" asked Otis Campbell, as I reluctantly gathered my skirts for climbing down.

"One and a half," Abraham replied. "Miss Reed is only going part way across."

We had the bridge to ourselves. The river flowed below, and the dark piney woods stretched on the other side. We could see the *Henrietta* nosing her way upstream, and heard her whistle. Midway the span, Abraham halted his horse, and we sat for a moment in silence. I was trembling, afraid to speak.

"Good things always end much too soon," Abraham finally said. "Dorcas, I hope you'll remember the lights and shadows. Look for the subtle things."

Then he jumped down and reached for my hand, and I climbed down too. It was chilly on the bridge, from the wind, as we stood there, Abraham and I. The steamboat whistled again. Abraham still held my hand, and I could feel the warmth of his touch spreading up my arm, as I looked into his eyes. I wanted to lean against him but dared not. I wanted to beg him not to go but dared not speak, and we stood there in silence for some few moments.

"Please convey to your brother my deep gratitude," he said at last. "This trip has meant a great deal to me. And, Dorcas—well, Dorcas, as for yourself...."

But he did not finish the sentence. Instead, he let loose of my hand.

"I'd better walk you back to shore," he said.

Thus Abraham Greene departed from Fayetteville. But scarce three weeks had passed before there came a letter from South Carolina, with half the page filled by a water-color sketch of Charleston harbor. From all indications, by the time that letter reached my hands, Abraham Greene had taken to the road again, so I could not reply.

The next letter came from Richmond, and I knew he was headed north. Then sometime in March I received a package that contained a lovely book of engravings, all flowers and birds, printed in England—the finest book I've ever owned. I have it still. The package bore an address in New York City, but whether his father's tailoring shop or Abraham's own lodging, I did not know. I was not sure whether my letter of thanks ever reached him.

Late in May, Abraham wrote that he was eager to set out traveling again. I gathered, from something he said, that there had been another letter in between, but it must have gone astray.

By then, of course, it was sultry and hot in Fayetteville, and people were already leaving town, escaping the vapors that bring so much illness. In summer, business was always slow at the Golden Sun, except for occasional travelers heading north. No one who could afford to journey elsewhere spent the summer in town. Even Rose-Ellen and I were making plans for our yearly visit up here to home. I can't say that it was actually cooler here—far from it, in fact—or the fever danger any less, but we tried to imagine it so.

I was grateful, though, that we were still at Fayetteville on that day, the twenty-sixth of June, when Abraham Greene appeared once more at the Golden Sun. This time it was James who greeted him. I was upstairs somewhere, folding linens, but when I heard a certain voice below, a shiver went down my spine. Immediately I rushed to the stairs, praying that what I thought I heard might in fact prove true.

There indeed stood Abraham Greene, explaining to my brother that his previous trip had exceeded all expectations and proved so profitable that he'd decided to do it again.

"Well, you won't find much picture-painting business at this time of year," I heard my brother say. "Most folks have already left for cooler climes."

"Still, you never know until you try," Abraham Greene replied.

This time Abraham made no effort to barter but paid for his first week's lodgings in advance, with cash. In another day or two he was painting the carriage-maker's likeness.

But this time around his work seemed to occupy Abraham less totally than before. I don't mean that he applied any less of his skill, only that he laid his paints aside in plenty of time to wash for supper, and he did not resume when the meal was through, though daylight continued for another hour or two. Instead, he sat on the verandah, talking to James and me, or making cat's cradle for my nephew Jeremy. Abraham made great sport with

76

Jeremy, who was six that summer, and almost every evening led Jeremy and me on a stroll to watch the setting sun.

I knew, plain as anything, that Abraham Greene was in Fayetteville because of me. He never said so directly, but I knew—and I reckon James did too. Every so often, in the midst of conversation, I'd glance up and find Abraham Greene watching me. Our eyes would meet, and my heart would leap. No words, but I knew.

I don't recall much else about that week—what I was sewing, for instance, or who else was lodging at the Golden Sun—but I do remember the blinding joy I felt at being with Abraham Greene again.

He'd been in Fayetteville a week when Saturday rolled around again. There'd been some extra rowdiness in town that afternoon. Two Negroes had been discovered missing, and folks were riled about that. Supper that evening was later than usual, and immediately we rose from the table, Rose-Ellen asked my assistance in putting the children to bed.

Then, when the boys were down, Rose-Ellen said she'd a notion to wear her sprigged muslin to church next day and would I help her alter the bodice to fit. Rose-Ellen had miscarried again some weeks before, and her figure had not entirely returned to its previous form. Naturally I obliged, though my thoughts kept skipping down to the parlor beneath me. As I ripped and adjusted seams, I listened to the sound of Abraham and James in deep conversation below. What were they speaking of? I could not hear specific words, but the inflection of Abraham's speech drew me like a moth to a flame.

I tried not to show my vexation as I stitched hurriedly, but I could not abandon Rose-Ellen to wearing a gaping dress. Curfew tolled and still I sewed, and soon I heard my brother James extinguishing the parlor lights below. I heard Abraham go down the front steps, out for his evening stroll alone. Reluctantly I retired without bidding Abraham goodnight.

The next morning, there was the usual bustle as we readied ourselves for preaching at Evans Chapel. I could not decide which bonnet to wear—since Abraham's arrival, I had taken to preening in unaccustomed ways. Though Abraham was not at the breakfast table, I did not think it strange.

But when we came back to the house at noon, I *did* expect to find him on the verandah. He wasn't there. Nor was he in the parlor or in the dining room, where the table was already laid. James and Rose-Ellen and our guests began to take their places, but I went upstairs to put my gloves away.

The door to Abraham's room stood open, and I could not resist peeking inside. The room was empty. Abraham Greene was not there. With astonishment, I realized that his port-manteau was missing as well, and his paintbox and easel too. The room contained not a trace of Abraham Greene, except a half-finished painting, still wet, leaning against the wall.

I rushed downstairs to the dining room, where James was waiting for me before commencing grace.

"Mister Greene's room is empty!" I exclaimed. "He's packed up all his things!"

"Yes," my brother said, "I believe he did indicate that he might be departing today."

"Well, he didn't tell *me!*" I said.

"It won't ten minutes after you folks done left for preaching that Mister Greene streaked plumb out of here," Delilah reported, standing in the doorway with a platter of ham. "He lit out so fast you'd have thought the Devil hisself was on his tail."

"Dorcas, please be seated," my brother calmly insisted. "Our guests are hungry, and their dinner is getting cold."

"Don't hold off on account of *me*," I replied. "I'm not hungry in the least!"

I was much too stunned to consider appearances and pride. I rushed out the front door and set out through town, half-running despite the heat. I headed straight for Clarendon Bridge. For some reason, I expected to find Abraham there, waiting for me in his gig.

Otis Campbell swore that no one had crossed that morning except for a red-headed Scotsman with his son along, but I did not believe him, and raced for the other side. I had reached the woods on the opposite shore when my brother caught up with me.

"Dorcas, get in this wagon this instant!" James called. "Stop making a fool of yourself where everyone in town can see!"

Dejected, I obeyed. James did not immediately turn the wagon around but remained in the hot piney shade. I sat there in my Sunday frock, too stunned to cry.

"I guess your friend Abraham is more honorable than I gave him credit for," James said after a while.

"What do you mean?"

"Oh, we had ourselves a talk last night. A frank and honest talk. It was Abraham who commenced it."

Scarcely able to breathe, I waited for James to continue.

"Well, it seems that Mister Greene had set his cap for you. I don't know how much of a surprise that is for you, but he came right out and admitted it to me last night. He said he hoped to prove himself worthy of your affection and regard. And, Dorcas, you *know* that I had to tell him it would never do. I don't care how fine a painter he is."

I looked at James in disbelief. Surely I had not heard him right? My brother, to give him his due, was too embarrassed to meet my stare.

"Believe me, Dorcas," James muttered, "it wasn't an easy matter to discuss—but my duty was clear, and I stuck to it."

"*Duty?*" I rasped the word.

"Yes, my *duty*. You are my own blood sister, and I'm accountable for your welfare. I can't, in good conscience, let some Yankee vagabond lead you off to Lord knows where—I can't assent to letting you be ruined that way!"

"Yankee vagabond! Oh, surely, James!"

"Taking up with a man like that, you'd likely starve. What if he was to up and die, and leave you penniless? How would you fare—way up yonder, apart from all your kith and kin?"

I said nothing, until James felt obliged to inch his way closer to the painful truth.

"Dorcas, Abraham Greene is not one of *us*. And I told him so, plain as I could. And you're not one of *them*, and never could be. Now that's just how it is, and you'd best accept it, without getting carried away with outlandish notions that simply will not do."

"Just because he's a *Yankee?*"

I still did not understand, until James spelled it out for me in words as plain as those he'd used with Abraham Greene.

"No, not because he's a Yankee. I'm not always partial to Yankees, I admit, but that's not sufficient cause to prevent you from marrying one. No, to speak bluntly—it's on account of him being a Jew."

My brother did not spit as he uttered that single syllable: *Jew*. He did not hurl the epithets that I've heard so many others use, but unspoken stones can also bruise and wound. Because as soon as James spoke that word—with all that his speaking of it implied—I knew that Abraham Greene was lost to me. An uncrossable chasm had opened up between us. Abraham Greene was a man of integrity and pride. How could he ever forgive my brother for what he said? How could he ever trust *me* again?

Because, yes, Abraham Greene was a Jew. He had never said as much, nor had I truly acknowledged the fact before—but when my brother spoke, I knew it was so. And knowing it did not diminish my love for Abraham one whit. But from that instant on, my love was stripped of hope and was wrapped instead in woe.

Even with all that has since transpired, even with Isaac Howell and all that *he* means to me, I still count as a tragedy the loss of Abraham Greene.

Abraham Greene was a Jew, born in New York City. And I was a Methodist, born on a backwoods farm—but a Quaker two generations before, and perhaps an infidel two generations hence. Was that sufficient cause to prevent us from joining our lives into one? I am no longer hopeful or innocent, but as long as I live, I shall never willingly assent to blind divisiveness. I don't care what others say.

Of course I wrote immediately to Abraham Greene, at the only New York address I had. I begged him to forgive my brother's unkindness. Most especially, I wanted him to know that my brother did not speak for *me*. I sent three letters, each a fortnight apart, but received no reply.

Eventually I managed to forgive my brother James. I knew he had acted on what he thought to be unselfish principle, that he had earnestly tried to consider my welfare, beyond what he thought would be merely passing pain. But my brother was wrong. He sinned in his judgment of Abraham Greene.

Never again did I hear word of Abraham Greene, and to this day, I do not know whether he's alive or dead. I do not know if he still paints likenesses, or if he ever married.

Several Jewish families live here in town. One of them runs a dry goods shop two doors down from Ike's store. He's a young man, not many years older than Abraham was back then, and he came here from New York City. I have often been tempted to ask if he's ever heard of a painter named Abraham Greene, or if any of his uncles and cousins know such a man.

But I've kept silent. All these years, I've never spoken to anyone the name of Abraham Greene, not for the past three decades, not since that fateful Sunday. My beloved husband has never heard of the man. The name Abraham Greene has never crossed my lips—until now, when I whisper it aloud in this dark attic.

Chapter Twelve

Saturday, November 17th, 1860

We were awakened this morning just before dawn by the sound of the fire bell ringing. It was Ezra Borden's house, over on the west side of town. It caught sometime in the night, and by breakfast Ezra and Betsy were homeless, and them with six children too. They lost everything they had except the nightshirts on their backs. Well, they did save their chickens, and the butter churn, which Betsy had mistakenly left in the yard the evening before.

I sent Lydia to find out what had happened, and she reported that Ezra and Betsy and the baby will move in with Betsy's brother, and the rest of the children will be parceled out all over town, until Ezra can get some part of his house built up again. I imagine folks will do what they can to help. I sent Lydia back this afternoon with one of our spare bedquilts, and two or three cooking pots that I seldom use.

While I'm up in this attic, I ought to search through these trunks for some of the clothes and toys that belonged to Ike's children. But those garments are so old-timey now that the Borden children would be reluctant to wear them.

Bad enough, being burned out of house and home without the added shame of looking like poor ragamuffins. Well, in a day or so I'll send to Betsy for her family's measurements and see if I can't stitch up a few little frocks. Might as well keep occupied as I sit by Ike's bedside. Perhaps it will free my mind from my own coming bereavement.

I never hear a fire bell without my stomach wrenching in alarm. I never smell smoke in the wind without an immediate sense of dread. That's because of what we all went through in Fayetteville. I feel it's my special duty to help burned-out folks collect their lives again. I feel it's the least I can do, after what *we* experienced.

It was the last Sunday in May, back in Thirty-One, that *our* fire broke out—not yet a full twelve months after my loss of Abraham Greene. I don't know why disaster strikes so often on the Sabbath. Maybe with so much praying, we get swept away with our own false righteousness. We rest too easy, so the Lord has to hurl down a lightning bolt and shake us up again.

It wasn't lightning, though, that started the fire that Sunday noon, but James Kyle's cook, fixing her master's dinner. Church was over. Everyone had done with public praying and returned to their separate dwellings to partake of the bounty with which the Lord rewards His chosen. At the Golden Sun, still in our Sabbath finery, we had just sat down to eat in the dining room. James had carved the capon and was inquiring of our guests whether they preferred white meat or dark, when we heard the fire bell ring, down at State House Square.

"For the love of mercy!" my brother said. "Rose-Ellen, you'd best take over the serving of this fowl. And I do hope it's a false alarm so I can get back and eat before you all have demolished this bird entirely."

James unknotted his cravat and tossed it over the back of a chair before grabbing the pair of buckets that always stood at our door. James, as a citizen of the town, was obliged to render assistance whenever the fire bell rang. Our guests, who felt no such duty, proceeded with their meal. But my own inquisitiveness flared up, so I rose from the table and went out to the front verandah.

It was oppressively hot, without a trace of breeze. I was suffocating in my stays and did not envy my brother the exertion of fighting a blaze. The Golden Sun stood some blocks west of State House Square, and all I could see at first was the rising smoke. There was only a modest commotion, I suppose because folks were slow in answering the summons. It's hard, when you're feeling leisurely and safe, to respond with haste to a sudden threat of doom.

I was still on the front verandah, debating whether to set out for a closer look or whether to go back inside and finish my meal, when I realized that the smoke had mushroomed higher and the fire bell had ceased. I could hear loud yelling and assumed that the fire had taken an unexpected turn. A Negro lad, about ten, was running along the street and shouting himself hoarse.

"Market's done caught! They wants you all to come!"

I rushed to relay this information inside, even as I reached for an apron to cover my dress—a white linen apron that was as black as a widow's garb before the day was through. Rose-Ellen, our guests, and the cook—Delilah had left our hire by then—raced after me down the street. A block from State House Square we encountered such confusion as I have never seen, before or since. I doubt if Hell itself can compare with what we experienced that Sabbath afternoon.

Our wooden State House was indeed ablaze, a solid tower of fire, as though it had been constructed of lightwood specifically for making a torch. And Mr. Kyle's fine brick house was burning too, and his kitchen and smokehouse, and also the dwelling next door and the store across the street. People were running everywhere, white and black, old and young. Some were trying to get the town's engine to pump, and others were leading their horses to safer ground. Women were in tears. Children were screaming, dogs barking.

The waterworks, in which we'd previously taken such pride, failed completely in our hour of need, so we formed a bucket line for hauling water from the creek. But what could buckets do against such a blaze? The moment we had a working chain from Hay Street to the creek, the fire broke through in another place, and we had to start over again. Fences were burning. Houses were burning. The harder we worked, the more the flames shot forth. I saw the Russell sisters toss silk dresses from an upstairs window, but the fire caught up with them, and those garments merely served as tinder.

We grouped and regrouped, losing more ground each time. I worked to the point of exhaustion. Back and forth to the creek I ran, dunking in bedsheets and quilts and then handing them on to be laid over someone's roof. Soot filled the air, and sparks rained upon us. My feet were blistered, my ribs bruised, but still I passed the dripping sheets to the Negro woman who stood the next in line. Once, my sleeve almost caught, but I knocked the cinder away just as the hole scorched through. I wished I could wade in the creek myself, but every drop of water was needed against the blaze.

I saw Storekeeper Duncan rush by, with his fiddle under one arm. Old Mrs. Tippingham darted back into her burning house and emerged again with a china teapot and one lone cup. It's amazing, in the hour of destruction, what risks some people will take to save a precious object—but far more treasures were lost than saved at Fayetteville that day.

Those of us defending the west end of town were not aware that the inferno also raged in other quarters. But that fire—the great Fayetteville blaze of Thirty-One—spread towards all the compass-points. The flames shot up each street that led from State House Square, until one fiery cross marked Fayetteville. We were helpless against the enormity of that fire.

How many hours did we struggle? Four? Five? Six? The town clock had been destroyed, and the sun seemed never to move but glared directly overhead, adding its heat to that of the flames. I doubt we could have fought much longer. Some folks had already deserted, although others had come in from the countryside to take their places in lending assistance. They said the smoke was visible from twenty miles away.

Then finally we managed to keep John Boomer's house from igniting. I think it was a combination of sufficient wet blankets on the roof and a fortuitous row of shade trees that slowed the progress of the blaze. There was also some shift in the breeze, though the Lord was apparently deaf to our beseechment for rain. Anyway, that victory marked the furthermost destruction along Hay Street, some three blocks from State House Square, where it all began—and scarce two hundred yards from the Golden Sun.

Gradually the flames began to die. Buildings already caught continued to be consumed, but there ceased to be any leaping ahead, and by twilight the awesome spectacle of fire gave way to a more somber scene.

Only then, I think, did the knowledge of our loss strike full upon us. Our lively, cheerful town lay wasted before us, one vast expanse of smoking ruins. Standing at the wagon yard, you could see clear to Cool Spring with nothing to obstruct the view except for a handful of trees, scorched bare, and all the blackened chimneys, useless against the smoke that still rose from the charred remains.

Nothing had proved too sacred for destruction—neither State House nor store, bank nor academy. Two churches were burned, and the two largest hotels. And hundreds of dwellings had disappeared.

Now, instead of roaring flames, the air was filled with wails. Families began to collect again. Mothers called out the names of their children. Masters took count of their Negroes. Our devastation grew particularized as one person after another tallied their loss. If a single burned-out family counts as a tragedy, then what words can describe a *thousand* persons left homeless in the space of an afternoon?

Even nightfall brought no relief because, exhausted though we were, there was yet more work to be done. Nearly a hundred folks took shelter at the Golden Sun that night—indeed, many of them stayed for a month or two. We allotted the beds to those who were elderly or infirm, and more than one dresser drawer served as an infant's cradle. People lay asleep everywhere you looked—on the verandahs, in the parlor, along the halls. The heat of May was a blessing then, because most of our coverlets had been lost in fighting the blaze.

Miraculously, no one died in that fire, although two elderly citizens expired in the next few days, an aftermath of fright. Our town was gutted, but our lives had been spared, and we took grateful notice of that.

And the Golden Sun remained, so that James and Rose-Ellen and me had much to be thankful for. Our linen supply was ruined, and we emptied our pantry of stored provisions to feed those under our roof, but in a peculiar way, our business actually improved as a consequence of that blaze. For the next several months, until the Eagle was rebuilt, all the stages that passed through Fayetteville arrived and departed from the Golden Sun. For weeks, all travelers who came our way—and some still did come—had to lodge with us, if they found accommodations at all.

Our personal loss was naught compared with those rendered destitute by the blaze, and I took cognizance of that. Yet I too was painfully robbed by the flames that consumed so much of Fayetteville that day. It was the miller's wife who called my attention to that fact. The fire had demolished a painting that Abraham Greene had done of the miller's oldest daughter. The girl had died of typhoid the autumn before, and now the family mourned not only their daughter but the loss of her likeness too.

With a shock, I realized that the fire had consumed almost all of the portraits painted by Abraham Greene. The mayor's house was burned to the ground, and likewise Judge French's house, and so it went. No more places remained where I could discreetly gaze at the work of my Yankee limner friend. Now even Abraham's paintings were denied me.

If the Lord Almighty intended that fire to teach us some spiritual lessons, then the blaze succeeded, because we learned to take nothing for granted. We learned that our most cherished possessions could be swept away in an instant, and that a person can fall from comfort to penury within the space of an hour. We learned humility. Our rugged pride was broken, and we acknowledged our dependence upon the whole of humanity. We learned to be grateful for each small kindness bestowed. Indeed, we were fully chastened.

Even today, the ringing of a fire bell brings me to my knees. Shivering in this attic, I feel it as strongly as I did three decades ago: the loss, the anguish, the shock and humility.

Chapter Thirteen

Wednesday, November 28th, 1860

This is a time of waiting. I sit by Ike and search for the slightest indication of change. I seize each flicker as a sign of hope, and I pray for miracles, but his condition remains the same. Each day is almost like the one before. Everything seems gray and continuous—day and night, day and night—as I sit beside my husband and helplessly watch his life ebb away.

My world is Ike's sickroom and this attic, where I take brief respite before resuming my vigil again. I do not participate in the swirling discussions that absorb everyone else in town. For weeks I have not stepped foot outside my own yard, so I cannot say whether folks' agitation has finally begun to subside or whether it's boiling up the more.

For me, there can be no advantage in the swift passing of time. I would hold back the minutes if I could and forestall the upheaval that lies ahead. I do not complain of the sameness or of staying cooped up inside. In fact, I wish this *were* a dull and ordinary year—one of those years when nothing occurs to distinguish it from any other time. But alas, it's too late for that.

When I reflect on the past, certain years stand out in sharp detail, even now, while others are lost in shadow. Thirty-One, for instance, I still view as a watershed, marked by that blaze roaring through the heart of Fayetteville. After that, events seemed to slide downhill and break apart, at least in a civic way.

If I were of an astrological bent, I'd look skyward for explanation of why so much went wrong in Thirty-One. Perhaps some movement of the planets set forth our disasters. That Negro, Nat Turner, up in Virginia, the one who led such a terrible spree of killing white people in their beds, claimed he had been given a heavenly sign. He said his orders came from the stars and from Scripture, though I cannot imagine the Lord Almighty consenting to the slaughter of some sixty white folks, not counting the black people who died—but then again, I would never have thought He'd allow such destruction as we had experienced at Fayetteville.

That bloody business in Virginia occurred the same summer as our fire, and I remember how news of the event scorched through Fayetteville anew, and gave folks something else to fear. Were the Negroes about to rise? Suddenly every black person in town, whether slave or free, had to be strictly accounted for. There developed much stirring and ferment. The Light Infantry began drilling more frequently, and yet more laws were passed to restrict what a Negro could do.

That was the year my brother hired a stableman and cook who were working to buy themselves free. They'd been with us four months when that great fire broke out, which led to a question about whether the arrangement could stand. Their owner, Mr. Joseph Creel, lost his house in the blaze and needed his money immediately so he could start to rebuild. James agreed to advance Cato and Bess the funds they needed to complete their own purchase.

Then that business happened in Virginia, and a great groundswell of objection rose against freeing Negroes, no matter what the reason. It was fortunate for Cato and Bess that their transaction had already occurred. Still, for safety's sake, they had to go up North somewhere, rather than stay and work out their debt at the Golden Sun. My brother consented to an I.O.U., and every summer after that, James received an envelope containing a few dollar bills. I don't know how much of that debt was cleared before my brother himself pulled up stakes from Fayetteville.

Dire circumstances marked Thirty-One, but the next spate of time has blurred in my memory. Nothing stands out to mark what transpired in Thirty-Two, or when Thirty-Three began. I sewed and I painted. My nephews grew older. Business was brisk in the autumn and slow in the summertime. In March, the daffodils would bloom, but I don't remember finding pleasure at the sight. In July, Rose-Ellen and the boys and I would make our annual visit up here to home and stay for a fortnight or so.

The years passed, that's all I know, and gradually our town began to be restored. Debris was hauled away, or put to use again, and new dwellings arose. Ironically, during those same years my services as a likeness-painter were requested more often than before. Somehow their awareness of loss made folks more eager to record their loved ones in tangible form. I don't know exactly how many likenesses I painted during those years, but it was dozens, and it gave me a certain satisfaction. Others might pile brick on brick or nail shingles on a roof, but I brought color and beauty into folks' lives again. It wasn't much, I realize, but it *was* something, and I was grateful to have it to do.

And then, without warning, one autumn afternoon in Thirty-Five, an urgent letter arrived from Isaac Howell. My sister Caroline was ill—consumption, the doctor feared—

and she was also expecting again. Ike was worried, and he wondered if Rose-Ellen or I could possibly come to nurse her, at least for a fortnight or two. Belle Yancey had sent them one of her Negroes for several days, but now it was cotton-picking time, and the Yanceys needed all their hands for that.

Ike's letter reached us about half past four in the afternoon, and long before daylight the following morning I came downstairs from my attic room, kissed my brother and Rose-Ellen good-bye, and departed. James had hired a special transport to carry me directly to Caroline. Most of the town had not yet awakened, and it was too dark to distinguish the shapes of the houses as we rattled through the now-familiar streets and into the woods beyond. I have never laid eyes on Fayetteville again.

My sister Caroline was in far worse shape than Ike's letter had indicated. I had never seen her so wan and thin, though the child she carried had already increased her girth. She was seized with coughing when I first saw her, and I waited in the doorway until she lay quiet on the pillows again. Apparently she had not heard the commotion of my arrival. Perhaps she'd been asleep—she slept a good deal of the time—but when at last she spied me, my sister burst into tears.

I used to wonder whether events would have turned out different if Caroline had miscarried the child at an early stage, the way Rose-Ellen was prone to do. But Caroline did not. Caroline clung to maternity even though it was clear that she scarcely had strength enough to sustain one person, much less two. Sometimes I ask myself why Nature holds folks to such harsh account. Caroline was wasting away before our eyes, and yet her body refused to relinquish the child.

Two days after Christmas she finally delivered a still-born child. By then, it was apparent that Caroline herself would soon expire, which she did some four weeks later. I am not a midwife—indeed, I tend to a certain squeamishness—but, between Rose-Ellen and Caroline, I had assisted at several births. This was the worst experience of all. Caroline was so weak that she could not expel the body of her child, small as it was, and it had to be dragged from her. Immediately the stillbirth was over, Caroline fell into a feverish sleep and did not awaken until late the following day. I thought we would lose her right then, but she remained alive—or partly alive—until the end of January.

I cannot express the shock of realizing that Caroline— my *younger* sister Caroline—might actually depart this earth. Caroline was eternal! James and Caroline and me— the three of us were eternal! But despite my protestations, I think I acknowledged that Caroline would leave us long before Ike or the children did. They were too close to Caroline. They saw her every day and did not mark the change as acutely as I did. Besides, they needed her too much to admit that Caroline might die.

When I think back to that autumn spent in nursing Caroline, I still see all the children, my nieces and nephews, with their various reasons for tiptoeing into their mother's sickroom. They would make some simple request that only added to Caroline's pain, at not being able to do whatever was asked. Lydia was then fourteen, and the littlest one, Rachel, was almost three. Dan, Sam, Essau, and Timothy were spread in age between the two girls at either end.

Essau was just learning to read—Caroline had begun teaching him the letters before she got so sick—and one afternoon he brought his primer and wanted his mama to hear him. Caroline murmured encouragement but was in fact so faint-headed that she let a mistake slip by. At that, young Sam pointed out Essau's error, and the two of them

94

commenced to argue, the way brothers do. I made both boys leave the room, and when I came back, Caroline was crying. She turned her head so I wouldn't see.

It's one thing, I quickly learned, to be Aunt Dorcas from Fayetteville, who spends two weeks every summer painting her nephews' likenesses and stitching frocks for her nieces—but it's another matter entirely to have the whole weight of a household resting upon you. My dying sister needed attention, much as she denied it. Nine persons had to be fed at regular intervals throughout the day. Clothes had to be laundered and the floors swept. There was a heap of hard work to do, in addition to providing consolation and cheer.

I have always prided myself on being willing to work—shiftlessness I cannot abide—and yet when I arrived here and took up residence in this house, I was scarcely equal to the task. Cornbread had to be baked and chickens plucked, and I was all thumbs. Not only did I not know where the skillet was supposed to hang or where Caroline kept her mortar for grinding sugar, I myself had not cooked a meal from scratch for a dozen years. I had grown used to the Golden Sun, where platters of food appeared on the table without my assistance. Though I might have been to market to purchase the fowls we ate, and though I'd stitched the cloth the platters were set upon, I had not actually prepared the meal itself. The kitchen and the wash-tub were not my concerns at the Golden Sun.

I wanted to assist my sister, to relieve her from worry, and yet on my second evening I burned the biscuits so bad that they had to be thrown away. I was awkward with the children too. I was not used to coping with a half dozen children at once. What do you say when the three-year-old refuses to go to bed? What do you do when the six-year-old comes home with a torn shirt and a bloody arm? I had expected to sit by Caroline, to feed her broth and wipe her brow—the way I do now with Ike down below—but I was *not* prepared for the turmoil of everyday.

I don't know how I'd have managed had it not been for Lydia, calm and helpful beyond her years. Lydia has always been a person of smooth common sense, and she came to my assistance many times those first few weeks, until I had learned my way around and certain household skills had become familiar again.

The children suffered greatly, but it was Ike who fared the hardest. He was beside himself with worry about Caroline, and at the same time he was trying to reestablish his store. Earlier that year Ike had decided to risk moving his store to *here,* to what was then just a small settlement, the earliest beginning of what has since become a regular town.

Back when we were growing up, some few miles south of here, only five or six families lived within the boundaries of what is now this town. This was only a backwoods crossroads before they started the railroad, but once it had been determined to put a depot here, a settlement began springing up around where that depot would be, and this became a headquarters for boarding the railroad men. At any rate, Ike had just relocated his store to here. Over the long haul that proved a sound decision, but at the time it seemed to be a considerable risk.

Not only had Ike moved his store, he had also assumed some debt for building this house, which was new that same year. This is now a comfortable house, two stories tall with verandahs front and back, but back then only the barest effort had been made to get the place fixed up properly. Caroline had just moved in before she took sick.

When I first arrived, Caroline and Ike slept in the second-floor room above the parlor. Ike still shared the bed with Caroline, consumption or not, but in another month he set up a separate cot so he wouldn't disturb Caroline's sleep. It was the doctor who insisted on that, and by then Caroline was too weak to protest, one way or the other.

An unspoken terror pervades a house where someone is dying. I well remember it from that autumn of Thirty-Five, when I was nursing Caroline, and I feel such a terror now, especially at night as I sit beside Ike below. My husband was once robust and strong—he's that way yet in my memory—and now he lies speechless and pale. I ask myself: How could this happen? How could such drastic change occur?

It frightens me to consider that with each breath he takes, Ike moves that much closer to the edge of the cliff. One day he'll take a final step and fall clean away from me. Isaac Howell will be no more. I try to imagine that fact, in preparation. I place my hand on Ike's forehead and feel its moistness and warmth. I listen for his breath, his faithful breath, as it's expelled from his nostrils and then sucked in again. I wrap my fingers around his wrist and feel the pulse still throbbing.

And I tell myself: One day soon this will cease—the breath, the pulse. I'll glance away for an instant, and when I look back he'll be gone.

Chapter Fourteen

Thursday, November 29th, 1860

It's been raining since early morning, a hard steady downpour that slows every once in a while but then whips up to speed again. Rain can be refreshing on a summer afternoon—a quick storm can clear the air and turn things bright again—but these winter torrents bring no comfort. They don't cleanse the soul but merely add to our despondency.

Only a fool, I suppose, would climb to this damp attic in such a storm. Yet here I sit, wrapped in a woolen shawl and a quilt, huddled close to an old tin warmer filled with embers. That's my lone concession to comfort, up here. I light no lamp to chase away the gloom.

There a great rush of water directly overhead—a noisy flow, as though many tubfuls of water were being sloshed onto the roof. I wonder if Noah and his kin, sitting in their ark, listened to the rain pounding overhead, the way I do now. Or did the bleating and braying of animals overcome the sound?

It rained for almost forty days the winter that Caroline expired. The rain commenced before Christmas, and then kept on and on. I don't believe we saw the sun more than three or four times between the middle of December and the last day of January. Every room in this house was cold, though we kept several fires going. It was all the boys could do to keep enough wood hauled in. The woodshed had developed a leak, so half of the firewood was damp and tended to smoke. I thought we'd all suffocate, between the mildew and the smoke. It's no wonder that our nerves were raw before the end.

It rained as hard as it's doing right now, the afternoon that Caroline relinquished her soul to our Maker. When death comes, those of us left behind may seek consolation with thoughts of a sunlit shore, across on the other side, but it is hard to evoke such visions when you stand in the pouring rain and watch your sister's coffin being lowered into a watery grave. Better to have died at sea than to take your final rest in a grave where streams pour over the side. It's a wonder that Caroline's coffin didn't rise and float away before the dirt could be shoveled back in.

We had a simple burial in the town's new cemetery. There hadn't been more than three or four graves dug there before Caroline's stillborn child and then Caroline herself were laid to rest. No churches had yet been built in this settlement—that didn't occur for another year or two—and Emmaus Chapel was without a preacher. Enoch Taber, our Justice of the Peace, read some Psalms aloud as we gathered at the graveside and bade farewell to my sister Caroline. We strained our way through a mournful hymn, and I couldn't help but recall our singing-school days and the sweet harmonies created by Ike and Caroline.

It was several days after Caroline's burial before I acknowledged to myself how drained and exhausted I was. I was overcome with fatigue—well, all of us were. I tried to bolster myself with the thought that I'd soon be returning to Fayetteville, which seemed eternally sunny in my mind. I would take up my painting again. In an effort to lift the gloom, I thought of the pleasure that comes from layering rich, bright colors upon a canvas.

But it continued to rain, and the children all took sick, and I knew where my duty lay. How could I turn my back on my sister's motherless children? How dare I think about the satisfactions of life in Fayetteville? Ike never said anything, one way or the other. He never came right out and asked me to stay. I suspect he was afraid to discuss the subject, for fear that would open the way for me to proclaim my intentions to leave.

At any rate, I stayed on, and I tried hard to restore this household to comfort. Everywhere I looked, there was something that had been neglected and that desperately needed seeing to. My nephew Dan had outgrown all his shirts—he was twelve, just entering his growing stage. Sam and Essau needed haircuts, and so it went. And even a brand new house collects cobwebs and dust. When the weather finally improved, I went about my mission with zeal, airing every quilt and washing every window to let the sunlight in.

At breakfast one morning in early April, Ike said that Will Yancey would send one of his Negroes that day to plow the plot behind the house for putting our vegetable garden in.

"Dorcas, when I come home at noon," Ike said, "I'll bring you some seed-packets from the store. I might even have some flower seeds around. I reckon we could use a few posies, after what we've been through."

He asked if I'd decided which vegetables to plant. In fact, I had given the matter no thought at all, but as soon as he spoke, I started making a list. That's how I learned for certain that Ike wanted me to stay. So I wrote James and asked him to send my paints and the rest of my things up from Fayetteville.

Thus, when the skies finally cleared in the spring of Thirty-Six, *I* was the one, not Caroline, who oversaw the planting of all the vegetables we ate that year. I was the one who planted rose bushes around the house and the wisteria vine that now graces our front verandah.

Well, the downpour overhead continues. I wish I could relieve this *present* sorrow by planting flowers, but it's November. Our winter has only begun.

Chapter Fifteen

Friday, November 30th, 1860

Death is fearsome, but when you're responsible for six growing children, you can't dwell upon sorrow for long before the living call for attention again. We all wore black crepe armbands, but gradually, almost without our knowing it, the sharpness of our loss became less acute. Each of us ached in our own way, but as the weeks passed, our wounds began to heal. We began to emerge from our gloom.

The weather helped. I've seldom known a more fulsome spring than Thirty-Six, as though Nature was trying to compensate for all those weeks of rain. The trees put forth leaves, and the birds resumed their songs—it was little Rachel who called my attention to that.

"Aunt Dorcas, come here and listen!" she demanded, pulling me by the hand out to the front verandah. Who can resist the sound of a mockingbird on a bright May morning? And who can resist the rapture of a child, listening to such a song? Limb by limb, we stretched ourselves, like a cat on a windowsill. We opened ourselves to the sun and took up regular living again.

I knew that our recovery was truly taking hold when Ike announced, one Saturday in early July, that he and the boys were going fishing that afternoon. Worms were dug from the vegetable garden, poles were found, and off they went, the five of them, with Ike a boy like the rest. I heard him whistling as they departed and took it for a wholesome sign.

I decided that the girls and I needed some pleasure too. We'd go berrying. I reckon we looked a sight, wearing our raggedest frocks, our sleeves rolled up and our aprons on, with black bands on our arms and black ribbons fluttering from our calico bonnets. We set out north of town and found berries aplenty. It was hot, but the heat was tempered by a breeze. It was a wonderful afternoon. We stuffed ourselves on berries and filled each of the baskets we'd brought. Rachel was worn out by the time we were done, so Lydia and I took turns carrying the sleeping child.

That evening I made blackberry cobbler. Pan-fried fish and blackberry cobbler—you can't beat that for a meal.

On account of the pie, I suppose, I woke up thirsty sometime after midnight. I threw aside the mosquito net—the mosquitoes were bad that year—and slid to the floor, careful not to wake Rachel, who slept beside me, or Lydia, whose bed stood against the opposite wall. It was a warm night, and all the windows were open. Somehow, I thought I'd die if I didn't have fresh water immediately, so I slipped into my wrapper, without even knotting the tie. Barefoot, with my hair unpinned and loose, I tiptoed from the room and down the stairs. It was pitch black—the moon had not yet risen—but by then I was accustomed to this house and needed no light to find my way. I went straight to the back verandah, where we kept the water barrel.

I drank one gourdful of water and part of a second—drank it slow, taking pleasure in each swallow. Then I leaned over the verandah rail to pour some water onto one of the rosebushes I'd planted that spring. That bush, just showing its first deep red bloom, was my pride, and I gave it particular care.

I stood up and turned around, the gourd still in my hand and then...and then Isaac Howell grabbed hold of me and pulled me tight against him! I had not seen him standing there in the shadows against the house. I could not really see him now but felt him rather—felt the naked chest I pressed against, felt his breath upon my cheek, felt his hand caress my hair. I dropped the water gourd and heard it break.

He kissed me. Not on the cheek, the way kinfolks do, but full on the mouth. I was startled—yet did not attempt to pull away. I had not been kissed that way before, not by anyone, and I cannot begin to describe how it feels to have a man hold you close and run his fingers through your hair, when you've lived unmarried—and untouched—for so many years. No one had ever told me how intense the pleasure of kissing can be. That's not a subject you can easily talk about, or at least folks don't. That night on the back verandah was a complete revelation.

Ike did not say a word as we stood there, pressed together for I don't know how long. Then he spoke my name just once. "Dorcas," he said, as though it had an unusual sound. Not "Sister Dorcas" or "Aunt Dorcas," the way he usually addressed me. Then he turned me loose and went inside. I stood there shivering, despite it being so warm, until I heard him climb the stairs. His door was shut when I tiptoed past, to the room I shared with his daughters. Lord, but you'd have thought I'd run for miles, my heart was beating so! I did not sleep a wink until I heard the first rooster crow, then drowsed for a while.

When Rachel began to stir, I arose from bed, albeit with great reluctance. During the course of one short night, everything had changed. I thought of feigning illness, but the children were expecting breakfast, so I dressed and went down to the kitchen.

I did not look at Ike all that meal. I was too embarrassed. And if he looked at me, I wasn't aware of it. Nor did we exchange any words, except those required for passing cornbread and ham, but there was nothing uncommon about that. We were not used to a great amount of conversing, Ike and me.

When breakfast was over, Ike said that he needed to fetch some object that was out to the Yancey place. I was surprised, because we'd been to Belle Yancey's for dinner only the week before. The boys were delighted and raring to go, but Ike said no, not this time, because he needed the wagonbed for hauling back whatever it was.

"Dorcas," Ike said, "are you free to accompany me? If I know my sister Belle, she won't forgive me, except'n I bring you along."

I knew I had to go, faint-hearted or not, so I changed my frock, and we set out. Ike was silent until we were well out of town. I sat there beside him, silent too.

Halfway to the Yancey place, Ike halted the horse. He turned to me and said:

"Dorcas, I propose to marry you, unless you've got some objections."

I sat there, my head turned slightly away, not looking at him. Who was this man speaking to me? Isaac Howell was suddenly more familiar and yet more a stranger than he'd ever been before.

"Dorcas, are you listening?" Ike said.

"Yes, I'm hearing every word," I whispered, my bonnet still hiding his face from view.

He took my hand.

"Well, Dorcas, will you marry me? Will you be my loving wife?"

"Yes," I replied. "Yes, I will."

I turned to look at him then, at Isaac Howell sitting so tall on the wagon seat. This was not the same Isaac Howell I used to admire, back in our singing school days, though the resemblance was strongly apparent. He was a most handsome man. I don't think I'd really dared to look at Ike since he'd married Caroline, some fifteen years before.

And what did Ike see when he looked at *me?* Instinctively I raised one hand to smooth my hair. At that, Ike smiled.

"Dorcas, you are a fine-looking woman," he said, "but I doubt you even know it."

Thus I assented to wedding Isaac Howell. We proceeded to the Yancey place, and Belle Yancey, when Ike announced our plans, embraced me like a sister.

We were quietly married in the Yanceys' parlor the first Sunday in August. All of Ike's children were with us for the occasion, and Belle Yancey had one of her Negroes serve cake and tea around. I had hoped that James and Rose-Ellen could be there too, but Rose-Ellen was expecting— one last futile time—and feared to venture from Fayetteville.

I have often wondered whether my life would have turned out like this, had we not gone berrying that day, and had I not baked that pie and developed thirst as a consequence. What if I *hadn't* gone to the back verandah and stumbled on Ike there? Would we have continued to dwell beneath this roof in the same staid way, until his children were grown and I was needed no more?

Or might some other encounter, equally unexpected, have served as the spark?

Chapter Sixteen

Saturday, December 1st, 1860

South Carolina, folks say, is raring to cut all binding ties and start out fresh again—and many among us here hanker to do the same. I reckon South Carolina figures that by setting out anew, she can avoid all shoals and sail in perfect happiness forever more. Folks say a convention's been called for three weeks hence, and that it's already foreordained what South Carolina will do.

I well understand that craving to start life over, unfettered by the past. I expect most anyone who's lived into their middle years knows that same yearning. We all want our scars removed, our burdens lifted. Don't we all pray for a chance to shape ourselves anew?

I myself had such a chance when I married Isaac Howell. My life was transformed in ways that I would never have imagined. You'd think the mournful circumstances that drew us together would have overshadowed any pleasures that Ike and I might share, but it was not so. Those early years of our marriage brought me happiness beyond any I'd ever known.

I was loved. I was chosen. I was Ike's cherished wife, and he was my own dear husband. I know folks thought it a marriage of convenience, that Ike needed a woman to take care of his house and children, and there I was. Indeed, I was glad to prove useful, in return for so much pleasure and delight. The house and children claimed my attention—but Ike claimed me too.

At first, I worried about being a woeful substitute for my sister, but gradually I understood that Ike had loved Caroline because she was Caroline, and he loved me because I was *me*. Never once, not even in those first few weeks, did he call me by my sister's name. We were clearly different in Ike's mind, and his love of her did not diminish the affection he felt for me—nor, I'm certain, the other way around. Perhaps it's strange, but from the moment I married Isaac Howell, I rejoiced in being tall, and thus different from Caroline.

Soon I realized that Ike was proud of the fact that I'd lived at Fayetteville. I had mingled with merchants and travelers. I think that when he married me, Ike caught the scent of town—and liked it. Ike had been a backwoods storekeeper. He'd dealt mostly with farmers, and I was different. I think he was tired of living cut off from everywhere, which was why he'd moved his store to here. He hoped the railroad would alter things, as indeed proved the case.

For Ike's sake, and for my own, I'm grateful that this town has thrived. Now, it's nearly as big as the Fayetteville I used to know. And Isaac Howell has grown apace. His rustic ways are smoother now; he's lost that backwoods edge. At first, though, I was sometimes aware of my husband's country style, not that it lessened my happiness one whit. I well knew that speech and manners don't always indicate the essence of a man.

That's why it always riles me when Yankees and foreigners pass through here and remark on our ignorance. I resent the way they call us crude. Mostly, I expect, it's a case of what you're used to. If you've lived in London all your life, then Boston can't help but seem paltry. And if you've come from Boston, then maybe it's only natural to look down your nose at Fayetteville. And if you've lived in Fayetteville...well, then it takes some adjustment to return to the woods again. My fortitude was sometimes tested those first few years, until this town expanded enough to compensate for the one I'd left behind.

Both Ike and I had adjustments to make, when we embarked on our life together, but for everything I gave up, I found new riches and pleasures. Ike took me into his life and held me close, and I opened my heart to him. Our happiness carried us through.

With the children, however, the adjustments weren't always so smooth. I had no desire to lessen their memories of Caroline. I felt an obligation to my sister in that regard. If anything, I tried too hard to keep her alive in their minds. I understood their reluctance at calling me *Mama*—that honor was rightly reserved for Caroline. But who was I to be? At length, habit won out. Aunt Dorcas I'd always been, and Aunt Dorcas I would remain.

I was never Aunt Dorcas to Ike, though. To him I was just plain Dorcas, or else "my wife." Nor was I ever his darling or his precious sweetheart, because those endearments had belonged to Caroline. *My blushing beauty* is what he'd whisper as we lay clasped together in bed, though with the lamp extinguished he could not tell whether I blushed or not.

My blushing beauty. My cheeks grow warm even now, as I speak those words aloud. I cannot help but blush, despite my years, at the sweet memory of what those words imply.

Chapter Seventeen

Sunday, December 2nd, 1860

I wouldn't even know today was the Sabbath, except for Jesse Spruill bringing his family to town. I was afraid this week's rain might ruin the roads so that he'd never make it in—but we'd scarcely sat down to breakfast before he pulled into the yard. I might have known that Jesse would come, no matter what, because he'd promised he would. Jesse is that kind of man. He's red-headed, stubborn, and true. He must have left home by daybreak, to get here as soon as he did. For Lydia's sake, I'm glad. She misses him, that's plain to see.

The two of them are sitting with Ike now, and I've slipped away to give them some privacy. I don't reckon Ike's lying there will keep them from speaking to each other whatever they've got to say—not any more. Even were Ike to notice, I doubt he'd do more than nod in a friendly way. He's long since reconciled to Jesse Spruill—though it wasn't always so.

It's astonishing to consider that Lydia's been married almost as long as me. I look on her as such an equal and a friend that sometimes I forget there's more than two decades between us, that she's young enough to be my daughter. Lydia has always acted old beyond her years, though I don't mean in a dreary way. Certainly during those first weeks of my marriage I relied more than a little upon Lydia's helpful nature. I expect I took her for granted, if the truth be known.

I enjoyed talking with Lydia while we did the chores, the way I might have done with Caroline. I expect I bored her to death with talk of Fayetteville, and Lydia, in turn, related various local happenings of the past half-dozen years. I was largely a stranger here, after so long away, and Lydia's observations proved useful to me more than once.

The summer that Ike and I were married, a new house was constructed directly across the street, in what had previously been a stump-riddled field. Oscar Culloway, a partner in the sawmill, built that house for his young family. Phoebe, his bright-haired wife, had only one child when they moved in, but she was also keeping her brother's son, on account of her brother's wife having died the previous autumn. Tommy was three, the same age as our Rachel.

It wasn't long before a regular back-and-forth developed between that house and ours. Phoebe would come ask my assistance in cutting out a frock, or maybe she'd want Lydia to help her turn a feather bed. Oscar Culloway owned two Negroes, but both of those were men, working at the sawmill, so Phoebe struggled with the household alone. She was about nineteen and had been married only a couple of years. She had her hands full, between her own infant and her brother's lively child, whose temper-fits, I expect, were mostly a manifestation of the poor child's grief. I wasn't of much assistance to Phoebe in the child-rearing department, being so new to the business myself.

Anyway a natural friendship blossomed between Phoebe and Lydia. In the afternoons Lydia began carrying her sewing or pea-shelling across to Phoebe's house, and the two of them would work together. Sometimes she'd take Rachel with her too, to play with little Tommy. Soon it was nearly every afternoon that Lydia was going across the street. Sometimes I marveled that the girl had strength enough to help both Phoebe and me, but mostly I was glad that she had such a pleasurable friendship.

Then one Sunday in November when we were fixing to go out to the Yancey place, Lydia asked my permission to stay home that day. Her cheeks were slightly flushed, and I worried that she might have a fever. I took nothing for granted, knowing how quickly life can be snatched away.

"Sugar, are you ill?" I asked, laying my hand on her forehead.

"No, of course I'm not ill," she answered in that matter-of-fact way she has. "It's just that Phoebe has company coming and has invited me to partake of dinner with them. I said I would, providing you and Daddy don't mind."

So we proceeded to the Yancey place, leaving Lydia behind. We got back late that afternoon. It was already dark, and Ike was annoyed to find that Lydia was not yet home. We'd hardly stepped into the house, however, before Phoebe Culloway came running across to say that she had a heap of victuals left, and why didn't we all come for supper. Ike was reluctant to venture again from home, but I accepted, because Phoebe clearly expected us to come.

In the Culloways' parlor sat Jesse Spruill, dressed in a homespun shirt that had a frayed collar and had obviously never seen the likes of an iron. It was the first time I'd ever seen him, but I knew immediately who Jesse was, on account of the strong resemblance between him and Tommy, his son—the same red hair, the same stick-out ears. But Tommy wasn't sitting with his daddy. He was sitting on Lydia's lap, and she'd clasped her arms around the child. I noticed that Lydia's cheeks were flushed again, and soon I ascertained why. Whenever Jesse Spruill glanced her way—which was fairly often—Lydia's color would deepen a bit.

Ike sized up the matter too and was not pleased. Sure enough, as soon as we were home again, he let it fly, and thus ensued the only raging fit that I ever saw him have. He roared and stomped in a way that would have been awesome to behold, had his anger not been directed at Lydia. The boys and Rachel had been sent to bed, and the three of us—Ike, Lydia, and me—held forth in the dining room. It was chilly in that room, which added to our discomfort, but Ike did not stop to light a fire. I had never seen him so furious.

"Who *is* that ragged yokel, casting his eyes on you?" Ike barked at Lydia. "And how long has such audacity been going on?"

"Why, Jesse Spruill is Phoebe's brother!" Lydia tried to explain. "He comes into town every Sunday to see his son—he's a faithful daddy that way."

"Well, I will *not* have you flaunting yourself before the likes of him! Hereafter, whenever he's over to the Culloways', you'll stay right here to home, where I can keep a watch on you!"

Tears sprang to Lydia's eyes. It was the first time I'd ever seen her cry, except when her mother passed away. Lydia was scarce fifteen and stood no higher than my shoulder, but in many respects she was a full-grown woman. That was clear in the way she faced right up to her daddy. Somehow, as she confronted Ike, she reminded me of a younger Caroline, and I felt a sharp twinge in my heart on account of it. Maybe Ike saw the resemblance too, and maybe that added to his anxiety. Must he lose Lydia too?

"Jesse Spruill is as honest and hardworking as any man I know!" said Lydia. "And he's certainly not the first farmer to wind up poor. What do you expect, struggling out yonder on his place all alone? Why, he doesn't even have a wife to patch his shirt, much less make him a new one."

"Well, young lady, that's not any business of yours!"

It was painful to endure, watching the two of them. Lydia's cheeks burned with fire, and her eyes sparkled in the lamplight.

"I want you to know," she said, "that if Jesse Spruill was to ask me to be his wife—which he hasn't—I'd accept this very minute! I would consider it a sacred privilege! I would view it as an honor!"

Ike was stunned, and Lydia pressed her advantage.

"Daddy, *you* found yourself a wife to soothe your sorrow, now didn't you? *You* found a mother to take the place of the one your children lost!"

Was a painful truth about to emerge? Did Lydia resent Ike's marrying me? But just then she turned and put her arm around my waist.

"And I'm glad for it!" she said. "So isn't it only natural that Jesse Spruill might want to do the same? Of course, he hasn't said a word to me yet, but if he ever *does* speak, I'll be right happy to listen—I can tell you that!"

I feared for an instant that Ike would forget himself and strike his daughter, but he did not. He seemed angry with me as well, convinced that I was part of a plot to bring Lydia and Jesse together. I bristled at his allegations, but over the next few weeks, I did in fact take Lydia's side more than once, because the better I came to know Jesse Spruill, the more I felt his worthiness, and the more I felt moved to speak on his behalf.

Because that November evening was not the end of our acquaintance with Jesse Spruill. The very next Sunday, after dinner, Jesse himself came knocking at our door, and he spent the entire afternoon with Lydia, under the watchful eye of her daddy and me. The next four Sundays were the same, and on Christmas afternoon Ike reluctantly consented to Lydia's betrothal.

By then, Ike had worked himself around to accepting the notion of Lydia's marrying, though he still wasn't happy about it. There were two things in particular that Ike held against Jesse Spruill.

The first was age: Jesse was twenty-seven, a dozen years older than Lydia and only eleven years younger than Ike himself. Ike was not prepared to have his daughter take such a leap ahead, though of course there's nothing unusual in girls marrying older men. It happens all the time.

The second thing Ike held against Jesse was that he had so few worldly goods. The house that Jesse carried Lydia to had only one room and was built of rough-hewn puncheons; it wasn't even up to the standards that I had known as a child. Jesse's house, about ten miles west of here, did not have a single glass windowpane, not back then. It hurt Ike to watch his own daughter slide backwards to circumstances that he himself thought to have left behind forever. Surely it's only natural for a father to hope for his children some measure of comfort and success.

Nonetheless, Ike finally set his objections aside, and Jesse married Lydia in the spring of Thirty-Seven, when the apple trees were in bloom. They have never starved for lack of food—one look at Lydia will tell you that—but they both work mighty hard on that farm for relatively small return. Still, they have managed. All their children are healthy and well. And Lydia seems content.

Chapter Eighteen

Monday, December 3rd, 1860

I missed Lydia after her marriage. It wasn't good-bye for-ever, but I reckon Jesse had made enough Sunday trips to last him for a while. And after Lydia's first child arrived—that was Nancy, born within a year—the trips to town grew even less frequent.

For the first time in my life, I was without the daily companionship of a woman friend. Caroline, Rose-Ellen, and now Lydia had all been removed from me. Of course, Belle Yancey was my friend, but I saw her only twice a month, and besides, there were certain differences between Belle Yancey and me. The Yanceys owned some fifteen Negroes, with all the privileges that such a position brings, while I was the wife of a tradesman.

Admittedly, though I lacked female companionship, I had gained a houseful of children, each of them different, each of them delightful in their way. Ike's sons were all fine boys, prone to no more than the usual boisterousness. And with little Rachel I developed a special rapport. She was a winsome child, always drawn to objects of beauty—that was something we shared.

I had gained the children and a husband I dearly loved. But with Ike I've never felt entirely free to parade all my wild opinions and moral notions. Ike's most comfortable with things that are obvious and well understood. He is steady and practical, not much inclined to mental speculation. He does not yearn for what *might* be. Still, never once have I questioned the wisdom of marrying Isaac Howell. Even with all that has subsequently transpired, I have no regrets.

And yet, as the months went by, I began to experience a certain lonesomeness. I was bored—but not from idleness, Lord knows, because I worked hard from sunup to dark. Yet even as my hands stayed busy with necessary chores, my mind kept wanting to break away to livelier matters.

The truth is, I was lonesome for Fayetteville, for the spirited conversations I once had known—and especially lonesome for the painting I used to do. Miss Dorcas Reed had been a spoiled creature for sure, occupying herself in ways that were far beyond the reach of Mrs. Dorcas Howell. Though I'm ashamed to admit it now, I chafed at the many constraints that running a household brings.

In my mind, I began to devise a scheme wherein Ike and me and the children would visit Fayetteville. We would stay at the Golden Sun with James and Rose-Ellen. And once we were in town, I was certain, some previous acquaintance would immediately ask me to paint his family's likeness. Naturally I would oblige, and thus I would again have the satisfaction of filling a canvas with color.

This daydream was ripped apart, however, by a letter from my brother James. It arrived the exact same week that Lydia's child Nancy was born—that would have been in March of Thirty-Eight. To my distress, James said that he was selling the Golden Sun and that he and Rose-Ellen and the boys were moving clear to Ohio. I could scarce believe the words I read and was still in a state of shock when, some three weeks later, James and his family passed through here, already on their way.

That visit was exhilarating, sad, and much too short, though James was obviously eager to proceed with his new adventure. Once he settled his mind on a matter, there was no deflecting James. I scarcely slept a night the whole time they were here. The minutes were much too precious to waste on slumber. I pressed James and Rose-Ellen for word of Fayetteville until I came near to annoying my brother, who wanted to be done with Fayetteville, for reasons that he never completely explained. Business at the Golden Sun had been slower than in earlier years, but my brother's disaffection seemed to stem from something besides commercial concern. I gathered there'd been some threat or incident, though James was never specific.

"Ohio's not cursed the way we are," he did say one afternoon. "I want my boys to grow up free of this evil that damns us all."

Those were strong words and led me to believe that James was migrating primarily on account of the slavery question. He was not the first person, white or black, to head west as a way of loosening this choke-hold around our necks. Back then, there was a regular stream of folks heading west, though naturally they weren't all questing for liberty.

It was a pleasure to see my nephews again. Jeremy and David had each grown a heap since I'd left Fayetteville, and my brother was rightly proud. Jeremy was fourteen, about the age of Ike's Dan, and David was the age of Sam. It was strange to realize that Jeremy and David, whose infancy I'd watched with daily care, would be lost to me in their older years—while with Ike's boys it was just the opposite. Ike's sons, whose lives I now superintended, had come to me with their infant days past and gone.

One afternoon James borrowed our wagon and took the whole passel of children along while he showed Jeremy and David where our homeplace used to be. I went too, and it made me sharply aware of all the changes wrought by the passing years. I longed to hear my daddy's forge again and my mama's spinning wheel, but those days were never to be claimed again.

I have wished a hundred times that, in the press of that brief visit, I'd taken one last likeness of James and Rose-Ellen and the boys. I actually made a start one morning and began a pencil sketch, but then laid it aside for the sake of preparing dinner. The days went by so fast that I never even finished that simple sketch. Still, I've kept that fragment all these years, and now it's all I have left of my brother James.

On the dreaded day when James departed, I worried immensely. I had heard so many fierce tales of Indians and such that I feared my brother would meet a gruesome end, but James only scoffed at my ignorance.

"Dorcas, you're way behind the times," he said. "Cincinnati is a full-scale city, and much advanced beyond what we know here."

He was right, of course, as his letters eventually proved. When he reached Ohio, James bought another inn, one that dealt in the steamboat trade, much like the Golden Sun. From all indications, he prospered and was satisfied. He used to write once or twice a year, and every Christmas he'd send me a packet of books, because he knew that many of those volumes weren't easily accessible here.

To my immense sorrow, I never saw my brother again. Rose-Ellen, however, was sent back here for a visit after young David drowned so tragically, in the fall of his seventeenth year. That was in Forty-Four, after the railroad was running. When Rose-Ellen descended from the cars, we scarcely knew her, she was so distraught with grief. All of us—Ike, Belle Yancey, and me—did our best to console her and to lift her spirits again, but it was no use. A few months after her return to Ohio, Rose-Ellen herself passed away.

James died two years ago, when his heart suddenly gave way. He is buried out yonder in Ohio, beside his wife and son. My nephew Jeremy still runs that Cincinnati hotel. He is married to an Ohio girl and has five children—all of them strangers to me. Sometimes I wonder whether Jeremy holds any sentiment for the state of his birth, or whether he's gone over entirely to the Yankee side. I wrote him some weeks ago about his uncle Ike's condition but as yet have had no reply.

These past few days I have dreamed of James and Rose-Ellen—and of Caroline—back in those early years when we were young and hopeful, living in our simple cabins beneath the trees. I see the flash of their eyes, and I hear their voices. Isn't it wondrous that someone removed from this earth, beyond all human sight, can continue to live so vividly in mind?

I earnestly pray that my dear Isaac, after his departure, will dwell with me thus in dream and memory. Else, how could I bear the loss?

Chapter Nineteen

Sunday, December 9th, 1860

When Dan stopped by yesterday to pick up his horse and carryall, we convinced him to partake of supper with us. He assented easily to our persuasion. Dan seldom declines a meal, which surely accounts for his girth. He had gone, the previous day, to Raleigh via the railroad for some urgent meeting in connection with that committee he's on, the one that's planning a secession rally here. I'm disappointed that Dan has chosen to move in that direction, and I'm glad that Ike wasn't conscious enough last night to hear about it all. Ike would never approve of the tearing asunder that some folks propose to do. At least, I don't *think* Ike would approve of the path his oldest son is taking—but then, these days you never know anything for certain.

I doubt that Dan himself would have moved to such an extreme, were it not for Tom Yancey's urging. Dan looks up to Tom and always has, even when they were boys. Mostly, I think Dan is simply enjoying the stir. His life isn't terribly eventful, and he finds amusement where he can.

At any rate, he was full of news last night. Various resolutions passed here and there. More resignations submitted up to Washington City, or rumors of the same. Dan is certain that the Union will soon split apart. He says there's no stopping it now.

You'd think the passing years would draw this Union closer together, instead of having the opposite effect. You'd think that all the railroads would tie this country together and hold things fast, like stitching to a quilt, but instead the differences now seem more acute than they ever were.

We take railroads for granted now. At the drop of a handkerchief, we send delegates to Raleigh or Charleston, or up to Washington City. Yet it was only two decades ago that the first locomotive snorted through this town. And what a celebration that was! I was there, waving my flag like the rest. From that time forward, the trains have passed through here each day, bringing travelers and merchandise. More than once have I been grateful for all that's occurred in this town, on account of the railroad.

Today you can purchase all kinds of crockery, shoes, and implements within two blocks of this very house. Ike's was the second establishment along Main Street—but not the last, although not every development brought prosperity to the door of *Isaac Howell, Gen'l Merchandise*. Indeed, the arrival of a certain shopkeeper nearly plowed us under. Ike had the local advantage, but the newcomer brought a full purse and a Yankee sense of enterprise. Mercifully, this town grew rapidly enough to accommodate the both of them.

The railroad's coming was momentous, but equally significant—at least in my estimation—was a quieter occurrence the following year, when Theodore Tucker and his brother Thomas arrived here from Baltimore. With them came Mrs. Thomas, a new bride, a young pretty woman with hair the color of tasseling corn.

The Tucker brothers established our first academy, in a small frame dwelling on the corner of Chestnut Street. My husband, I'm proud to say, was one of the first men in town to support the academy. Ike wanted his sons to improve their station in life. I had spent many hours in instructing the boys, and Ike the same, but neither of us were familiar with rhetoric, Latin, or geography. Plain reading, writing, ciphering—that's all that Ike and I could impart.

When school opened in the fall of Forty-One, Ike enrolled all four of the boys, and not only for the basics but also for all of the "extras" that the Tuckers offered. Ike insisted that his boys seize all opportunities, and heaven hang the cost! Well, the cost was considerable when multiplied by four, and hard cash was sparing to come by. We had to pinch and sacrifice in every imaginable way.

Will Yancey also enrolled his Tom in the Tuckers' academy, and Ike and Will worked out an arrangement wherein Tom would stay here in town with us. In exchange, Will would pay part of the fees for our Dan. That worked out fine, though it meant I had another mouth to feed. Fortunately I didn't have to do Tom's laundry, which was taken home each weekend for one of the Yancey Negroes to wash.

You cannot imagine the difference that the opening of school made within this household—not to mention within this town. Shortly before nine every morning, the entire passel of boys would stampede out of here, and then upon this house would descend a golden, blissful silence. You could actually hear the ticking of a clock. You could follow a complete sequence of thought, without interruption. Rachel and I could perform our chores in peace.

Rachel was seven that year and beginning to help around the house, though she already took pains to avoid any dirty tasks. It was during that same year, when Rachel and I were home so much alone, that I most enjoyed the mothering of a child. Rachel was so sweet and fair, with her sunny curls and soft rosy cheeks. I began to teach her needlework, the stitching of feathers and flowers, and

Rachel had an uncanny ability for selecting colors and patterns, even that young. I suppose my instruction in the use of a needle has aided Rachel over the years in keeping finely attired, but my other teachings—in matters of heart and soul—apparently proved inadequate to the life that's been Rachel's to lead.

It was on account of the Tuckers' school that I took up painting again. The Tucker brothers called on us one evening, shortly after school began in that fall of Forty-One. It was something to do with cash on the barrelhead, as I recall. Young Mrs. Thomas was not along, and I don't remember exactly why I myself was in the room. At any rate, Mr. Thomas Tucker remarked upon the likenesses that hung on our parlor walls, assorted versions of Ike's children: young Lydia at the age of four, dressed in a bright yellow frock, and each of the boys as little chaps. I reckon I'd grown so accustomed to all those painted children that I'd plumb forgotten what a stranger might see.

"You have some mighty fine portraits here," said Mr. Thomas Tucker. "I can tell the family resemblance clear as anything."

"My wife did all those likenesses," Ike replied. "She has a regular knack for it, and I wish to goodness she could be persuaded to take up painting again."

Lord, but what a shot pierced through my breast at Ike's words! I'd never had the slightest notion that he cared for my paintings, one way or the other. He'd never said a word to me. Yet he sat there boasting of my skill. I nearly dropped the teacup I was handing to Mr. Theodore. Despite my joy and embarrassment, I managed to control my voice enough to speak.

"Merciful heavens, Mr. Howell," I said, "you forget these gentlemen have come from Baltimore. I'm sure they know the difference between real paintings and *my* poor humble work."

124

"Well, I don't claim to be an expert on art," Mr. Thomas said, "but I know what I like—and I do admire your work. I profess to enjoying a bit of color here and there. In fact, if I had any gift for it, I'd be tempted to take up painting myself."

But then his elder brother, Mr. Theodore, brought the conversation back to the subject at hand, and there was no more mention of painting that night. Still, that proved to be a dangerous evening, because from that time forth, the notion of painting was rekindled in my mind and soon burned with an intensity that came near to consuming me. My craving to paint, thus renewed, would not be laid quiet again, no matter how sternly I tried. With one of the boys' slates, I began to sketch out scenes and fragments of scenes—an eye, a hand, a tree—trying to regain my skill at blocking out a shape. Midway some household task, I'd even start drawing in the air with my finger, tracing a line visible only to me. More than once Rachel came upon me, acting the fool that way.

"Aunt Dorcas, what you squinting at?" she'd ask.

"Oh, it's nothing, child. I'm just drawing me a castle in the air."

Then I'd laugh and move ahead with my work, thankful that some things make sense to a child that a grownup would never understand.

During those same weeks I developed a wild, immoderate yearning for color, for every sort of hue. It was as though my eyes were starved and required the nourishment of reds and golds. Fortunately it was autumn, and I could fill the house with jugs of bright-colored leaves and baskets of apples—else I might have gone stark mad. I rearranged every object in this house, shoving the furniture every which way, trying out new perspectives, so that it's a wonder Ike and the boys didn't get seasick, from the topsy-turvy of it. I even set up my dyepots, and within the space of a single day I had transformed half the curtains to a deep indigo.

It was during that same time that I asked Ike to order me a length of ruby silk—though truthfully, I should have been ashamed to request such a luxury when all our financial resources were more than allocated to the boys' schooling. But Ike, my dear husband, humored me, and in a couple of weeks that silk arrived. Immediately I stitched up a red silk bonnet that set me off from everyone in town, and a red silk shawl to match. My Quaker forebears would have turned in their graves, could they have seen me traipsing along with that bold bonnet atop my head, but I didn't care! I expect it caused more than a little comment in this town—in fact, I know it did—and it may even have given my husband some moments of embarrassment. If so, he never acknowledged it. Folks have long since got used to seeing me in such attire, because through all subsequent years, until now, I've never lacked for a red silk bonnet to wear. When the first one wore out, I made me another, and so it went.

One day, in the midst of those passionate, crazy weeks in the fall of Forty-One, it plainly occurred to me that all my fuss and fury had not supplanted my craving to paint. *That* longing had not abated one particle. I finally realized that if I wanted so badly to paint again, then paint I must, and I decided to do a likeness of Rachel as Ike's Christmas present. I don't know why the idea hadn't sprung up before, since Rachel was the only one of Ike's children *not* to have been painted by me. The amazing thing is that as soon as I made that decision, my heart grew calm again.

The likeness would be a surprise. I enlisted the secret aid of one of Ike's merchant rivals to procure for me the necessary canvas and paint. From this attic I dug out my palette and brushes. For an easel I had to improvise, using a kitchen chair.

I set to work. Every morning, after the beds were made and the dishes done, Rachel would dress in her Sunday frock—something she liked to do—and pose in the parlor, close by the front window, so the light fell upon her face. Her frock was robin's egg blue, and I tied a coral ribbon in her hair and gave her a blushing pear to hold, though by the time that portrait was done, we had gone through three or four pieces of fruit, and in the end I had to paint the pear from memory.

It took me far longer to paint Rachel's likeness than I expected. For one thing, I couldn't paint but an hour a day, and when there was laundry or baking to do, I couldn't spare even that single hour. For another thing, my eye was not as certain, nor my hand as deft, as in the past. It had been five years since I'd taken brush in hand. Some treasures, once laid away, will stay intact forever, but such is not the case, I fear, with our highest skills and attainments. Our talents are too fragile. They wither and disintegrate, if set aside for too long.

At any rate, the paint for that likeness of Rachel did not flow easily upon the canvas. I had to struggle and work, to sketch and adjust, and more than once I came close to giving up in despair. As a consequence, that likeness was only partially complete by Christmastime, and the paint was too wet to be wrapped like a regular present. I hid the canvas up here in this attic and fetched it down when the moment for gifts arrived.

Ike was delighted. Half-finished or not, he propped that canvas on the mantel and expressed his admiration repeatedly that Christmas Day.

I have since understood that Ike, in the true spirit of love and companionship, had long wanted to share in the painterly side of me, a part of my nature that since our marriage had never unfolded before him. That painting of Rachel, aside from its family significance, was for Ike a token of sharing. It meant that I held him *worthy* of such a gift. There are some folks, I have discovered, who would never dare to purchase an item merely because of its beauty but who, for that very reason, find exceptional pleasure whenever such an item is thrust upon them. My husband Ike is such a person.

At any rate, Ike's enthusiasm served to encourage me, and I set to work with renewed intensity. Of course, now that the secret was out, I didn't have to hide my paint-smeared rags, so the pace went a bit faster.

A week or so before Rachel's likeness was finished, Mr. Thomas Tucker and his wife Eleanor came to call. It was late one Friday afternoon, when Ike was still at the store, and I was peeling potatoes for a stew. I ushered the Tuckers into the parlor and sent Rachel scurrying to boil some water for tea. Rachel's likeness, such as it was, stood propped upon a chair, where I'd worked upon it that day. Mr. Thomas Tucker and his wife peered at it closely.

"Your daughter is a lovely child," Mrs. Thomas said.

"Your husband told me you were painting this," said Mr. Thomas. "In fact, that's why we're here."

Mr. Thomas then inquired whether I would paint likenesses of himself and his wife—two separate portraits, to be done in oil, and of an equal size. In exchange, he offered to lower the fee for our boys' instruction the following term. Naturally I agreed in an instant, delighted that I could be of financial service to Ike—and, most especially, glad to have a good reason to continue holding a paintbrush in my hand.

I worked all spring on those two portraits, and the Tuckers seemed happy with my work—but not so happy as I, who felt finally restored to my whole self again. With a husband *and* painting, my bliss was complete.

Chapter Twenty

Monday, December 10th, 1860

Once I commenced painting again, there was no stopping me. I vowed that never, except for the direst emergency, would I let a week slip by without applying my skill in some way. And indeed, I kept that promise throughout all of Forty-Two.

When the Tucker portraits were done, I embarked upon a painting of Belle Yancey. And then, using Ike as a go-between, I approached the owner of our new hotel to suggest that his establishment might be improved by the addition of a grand landscape scene. Ike, I admit, had mixed feelings about that endeavor. He was proud of my painting but reluctant to have me accept cash wages, lest *he* be thought unmanly for allowing such a thing. However, he consented to barter as a sufficiently modest solution, and I finally did the job in exchange for triple the amount of paint and canvas I'd need.

Taking on that hotel job was nearly more than I had bargained for, between the chores of summer and the oppressive heat, but I forced myself from bed an hour early, and I planned every minute of my day. I'm afraid my household suffered. Fewer cakes and pies were baked, and the boys complained of the lack. The mending piled high in my basket, and often I sat up late and stitched by candlelight. My painting placed a strain upon us all, but my dear husband was exceedingly patient.

And then that autumn, I mean the autumn of Forty-Two, the Tucker brothers decided to add a female branch to their academy. This town buzzed with gossip of the new development. Our Rachel was anxious to take her place among the young ladies who would be privileged to attend—even then, Rachel had sharp instincts for what a fine lady should do. There was some question, however, whether Ike would enroll her. It's not that Ike objected to his daughter's refinement, but simply that our resources were already stretched too thin, and Ike felt a greater obligation to his sons.

The dilemma was resolved when Mr. Thomas Tucker came to call again. The female academy was his particular domain, and his wife was scheduled to offer the instruction in needlework and drawing. But now Mrs. Thomas found herself in the family way with their first child, and it would be unseemly to teach young ladies in such a condition, or so Mr. Thomas felt. He was in a dither. It was already September, the advertisements had been distributed, and enrollments were coming in. In short, he asked me to substitute for his wife in art and needlework.

I was gratified to have my skills acknowledged in such a public way, and Ike readily consented when it was determined that my teaching would lead to a waiver of fees—not only for Rachel, in the female department, but for Essau and Samuel too. Thus in the autumn of Forty-Two I embarked upon a new occupation: housewife, painter, and instructress.

Did I think I was busy before, with never a minute to spare? Well, that autumn I was ten times busier than previously. The days went by in a whirl. In the mornings I rushed through the necessary chores, and immediately after the noon meal I hurried out the door with the rest, my workbasket on my arm. Mondays, Wednesdays, and Fridays were devoted to needlework, and Tuesdays and Thursdays to the brush and pen. There were twenty-seven young ladies, of various ages, enrolled at the Female Academy. You cannot imagine the frenzy of directing the progress of twenty-seven cross-stitched samplers, or twenty-seven watercolor paintings of a gently flowing brook. But I loved it! Every single minute!

Then, as the day drew to a close, I rushed home to my kitchen again, to the chores left half-done. I drove myself with fury, trying to keep up with everything at once—the house, the garden, the food, the clothes—lest Ike and the children suffer in some way. *And* lest Ike protest my new occupation.

Time passed swiftly, until the second Sunday in January of Forty-Three, which proved to be a fated day. It was chilly, with gray skies and a strong wind—uncomfortable, but without the misery of rain. Belle Yancey had invited us to dinner, and I feared that the weather might keep us at home, but immediately breakfast was done, Ike hitched up the wagon and was ready to depart. Truthfully, I was glad to proceed, because I always looked forward to Sunday dinners at the Yancey place. It was a pleasure to eat a meal that I myself had not prepared, and then to lay my fork upon the plate, without giving thought to a panful of suds.

Belle Yancey lived in comfort. Her husband Will was not a man of great wealth, by any means, but Belle always served a tasty meal, and this dinner was no exception. Will carved up the fowl, and one of the Yanceys' Negroes handed the plates around. I gave it no special thought, although twice Belle admonished the girl for serving too clumsily. Belle was always particular about such things.

The dishes were at last cleared away. I noticed a sort of quickening in the room, a wink here or there, but attributed it to some tomfoolery on the part of the boys. Then the serving girl appeared again, bearing a lovely cake.

"You can set that cake in front of Miss Dorcas here," Belle directed.

The girl did so, but seemed a-tremble and ready to flee, as though that cake might explode and destroy us all. I realized then that the cake was intended for me—because my forty-third birthday was two days hence.

"Just stand right there," Belle said, with a gesture to the girl. "Now, Isaac, don't you have something to say?"

Ike rose to his feet.

"Happy birthday, my dearest Dorcas!" he said, with a little bow towards me. "And may you have many happy returns!"

Everyone cheered, until Ike held up his hand for silence.

"Now, Dorcas, in honor of this occasion, I have a surprise for you," Ike said. "I have a gift for you that will make your life easier in the years ahead—a gift that will lighten your burdens and give you more time to paint. Do you think I haven't noticed how hard-pressed you've been?"

I wondered what new contraption my husband had stumbled upon. An apple-parer? A new kind of rolling pin? Since the railroad was finished, all sorts of drummers passed through town, selling all manner of things. I waited for the package to be laid before me, but instead Ike flung out his hand.

"Sarimony, give a curtsy to your new mistress!" he said.

I did not comprehend at first but saw that the Negro serving girl, standing beside Belle's chair, was bobbing up and down, like a cork upon the sea.

"Yes, Missy! Yes, Missy!" the frightened girl stammered.

"Ike, what is all this about?" I asked with a laugh.

I thought it must be some skit or mummery performed in my honor. Often, I do confess, I lack sufficient wit to catch some meaning or joke that others grasp in a flash. This, I assumed, was such a time.

"Well, Dorcas," Ike explained, "you are a truly fine painter—and a fine teacher too, from what I hear tell. I am *very* proud of you, and I don't want you wasting your talents on laundry and such, no more than you can help. So, I've bought this here girl, and I'm giving her straight to you!"

To this day, I can hear Ike's speech ringing in my ears and see the loving look upon his face. I was overwhelmed by Ike's love and his sweet generosity—it moves me yet— but I was also appalled at what I slowly began to realize: *My husband had purchased a Negro slave and was giving her to me!* I was honored and betrayed in the exact same instant. Didn't Ike understand my feelings upon this matter? Didn't he know that, like my father before me and like my brother James, I viewed the trading of human flesh as an un-Christian blight? But, in fairness, how *could* Ike have known? It was one of those private beliefs that I'd grown accustomed to leaving unexpressed, lest I strike a hornets' nest.

For the first time that day, I truly looked at the serving girl. She was *not* one of the Yanceys' Negroes. I had never seen this girl before. She was young, short, and buxom, with a broad face and dark skin—too dark to be a mulatto, yet there seemed to have been some dilution of her African blood. Her head was wrapped in a clean white rag, and she wore a new gingham dress, the only respectable garment, as it turned out, that the girl could claim.

"What's your name?" I cautiously inquired.

"Sarimony, Missy."

She spoke so slow that I thought she said "Sarah Mooney," and indeed I called her Sarah all the first week, until Ike showed me the bill of sale.

"Well, Sarah, how old are you?"

"Don't know, Missy," the girl replied, holding her hands beneath her apron.

"She's eighteen," Ike interposed, "or at least that's what they said."

He had bought her, Ike explained, from a small plantation some few miles away. She had been a field hand and came fairly cheap, as Negroes go. It was Will who'd told him about the sale, although giving me a Negro had been entirely Ike's own idea. He wanted me to know that.

"Why, Sister Dorcas, you're white as a sheet!" Belle Yancey exclaimed, clasping my hand. "I hope you've not caught a chill!"

"My wife's plumb took by surprise," Ike said. "She's not accustomed yet to the notion of being waited on—but she'll get used to it soon enough, I reckon."

It's astonishing to me, how you can awaken some morning, expecting an ordinary day, and yet in the course of several hours some word will arrive, or some event occur, that turns your life in an entirely new direction, a direction that you had never anticipated before. So it was that January Sabbath. During the course of a single meal, on the eve of my forty-fourth year, I became the mistress of a full-grown Negro.

I'd had no say in the matter. I had taken no step of my own volition. I'd had not the slightest inkling of what was about to occur—and yet my husband's gift has irrevocably shaped every single day that has since transpired. The consequences of that gift can never be reversed. The weight presses upon me yet.

Chapter Twenty-One

Tuesday, December 11th, 1860

Most everyone agrees that it's our "peculiar institution," more than any other thing, that is wedging this country apart. Over the past dozen years one question has grown sharp and distinct: *slave or free?* Yet I wonder if it's as simple as that. Sometimes I suspect that the Yankees, with moral holiness, look down on us specifically *because* there are so many blacks among us, whether slave or not.

I have never been up North, but I understand that up *there* dark faces are not a common sight—whereas down *here*, black folks live all around. Negroes, owned and free, shape our terrain. They grow among us as common as the trees—and, like the trees, we scarcely notice them, though we always know they're there.

But viewing blacks as part of the landscape is one thing, and bringing an eighteen-year-old Negro girl into the bosom of your family is another matter entirely. My private beliefs on the slavery question aside, Sarimony's ignorance and sullenness proved a great shock to my system. Previously, my only real experience with Negroes had been with those at the Golden Sun, persons not only free but also skilled and competent. I was unprepared for the task suddenly thrust upon me, although Belle did try to warn me that Sunday afternoon.

"Sister Dorcas," she gently advised. "I expect you'll soon discover that owning servants is not entirely a blessing. Your girl's going to need right much training, and you'll have to be firm."

Belle did not speak the half of it. Mrs. Harriet Beecher Stowe's Topsy and Miss Ophelia were no more awkward a pair than Sarimony and me. The first question was where the girl would sleep. Ike had given no thought to that, so I fixed a pallet on the floor of Rachel's room. After that first night, however, Rachel pitched a fit, so Sarimony was forced to sleep in the kitchen, at least until spring, when our back shed could be transformed into a suitable human abode.

I was quickly disabused of my notion that every Negro female knew how to cook an edible meal. Sarimony could chop cotton, but she had only the rudest kitchen skills. Hoe cake she had mastered tolerably well, but that was the extent of it. The coffee she made was bitter; the chickens she roasted were scorched and raw at once. And as for pie dough...alas! My patience wore out, and I abandoned all attempts to teach the girl the art of the rolling pin. Sarimony washed dishes, but not without chipping them. She scrubbed the kitchen floor but inevitably missed a streak. She did the laundry but ruined my best petticoat.

Indeed, supervising the stitchery of twenty-seven young ladies proved not half the challenge of overseeing Sarimony's work. More than once I snatched the spoon or the mop away and did the task myself. Was the girl demented? Was it true, as many folks claim, that a Negro's mind could never advance beyond the most humble attainments? Or was Sarimony simply stubborn? She never budged an inch, no matter how hard I pulled and shoved.

She stood her ground as though protected by an impenetrable shield, but whether of malice or stupidity, I could not tell.

All through that winter, well into spring, I seethed with frustration. Owning a Negro, I discovered, did little to lighten my burdens and give me more time to paint—far from it! Instead, the household that I had worked so hard to maintain was slipping out of control. Competence and order were giving way to chaos. I could not count on finding any single object in the place it was supposed to be. The milk curdled, and my temper too.

The worst of it was that there was not a living soul to whom I could express that frustration. Ike was blind to the struggle occurring within our house. He had done his part. He had bought the girl and given her to me, and I resolved to bite my tongue in two before I'd ever speak a word of ingratitude. More than once, as I verged on complaint, I brought myself to heel again with the awareness of Ike's love. Ike respected me, and my painting too—and I would *never* forget how blessed I was in that.

It was not long, however, before I realized that Sarimony was wrecking a damage upon us far worse than broken crockery. The children began to act as if Sarimony's presence meant that they were now free of all previous chores. Pick up their clothes from the floor? No, Sarimony would do that. Fetch water from the well? No, such a task was now beneath them. Soon I had to contend not only with the insolence of my servant girl but also with that of the four boys and Little Miss Rachel besides.

Sarimony, to my indignation, made a great show of catering to the children's whims. I began to suspect she did it on purpose, as a way of spiting me, but of course a child's chores are much easier than those a grown woman must perform.

However, more disturbing than the laziness of Ike's children was the *pride* they soon displayed at having a Negro attached to our household. At first, I laid it to the influence of young Tom Yancey, still boarding with us. I knew that our boys had felt inferior to the Yanceys for not having Negroes to order about, but soon I realized that even Ike had felt that way. To my dismay, I realized that Ike had deemed himself less worthy than Will Yancey. This was not a matter of financial status but seemed to encompass basic human respect as well. In truth, Ike's notion was a common one, shared by almost everyone—and still is.

At any rate, for weeks we struggled together, Sarimony and me, locked in a dance of mutual distrust and antipathy. Then came spring, and at supper one night Ike mentioned that he'd made the usual arrangements for having our garden plowed. Tending a good-sized garden was yet another burden on my precious time, and I did not look forward to it that year, especially with the boys' new-found disdain at helping in any way. I dreaded having to nag them to weed and hoe.

But that same night, Sarimony came to me with a request.

"Missy, I be glad to take on the doing of that garden. I be right used to planting and such."

I was plain astonished. Was this *our* Sarimony, actually volunteering for some task? I hesitated to trust her. Had she yet proved capable of doing *anything* right? Dare I risk the family's nourishment? Wouldn't the garden be just another excuse for shirking her household duties?

At length, however, my craving for painting time won out, and I turned over to Sarimony all the packets of seeds. First, though, I recited sufficient instructions to confuse the best of minds—and had the distinct impression that Sarimony absorbed not a word of what I said. She stood there, hands on her hips, her turbaned head tucked down, and never once looked me in the eye. Although she muttered "Yes, Missy," at proper intervals, I might have been talking to the moon, for all the response I evoked.

But I gave her the twisted papers of seeds and turned her loose, then marched out to the Tuckers' academy. All afternoon, as I helped my young ladies neatly cross-stitch flowers, I worried about the disaster then occurring in my own back yard.

When the afternoon was over, I rushed home to inspect the damage. Sarimony was still at work, and she was singing a gospel tune—actually singing aloud—as she counted out kernels of seed corn and planted them by threes. The garden was mostly in, except for some few items awaiting a more suitable phase of the moon. Sarimony had even devised a complex pattern of sticks and stones to keep track of what was planted where, to mark the salad from the peas.

The amazing thing is that from that day forth, a new Sarimony was revealed to me. Although the indoor Sarimony improved her kitchen habits not one whit, she had much less tendency to sulk and pout. The *outdoor* Sarimony was a different creature entirely, as neat and industrious as anyone could wish. At daybreak I'd see her out in the garden, pulling grass or gently training a vine in the way she wanted it to go. Sometimes, thinking herself unseen, she would toss her head back and stretch her arms high in a stomp or a dance, as though exalting in her own strength.

That garden became Sarimony's private estate. She cleverly planted pole-beans around an open six-foot square, training the vines to form the "walls" of a room. Sarimony even put a rough pine bench in her bean-vine room and would rest out there from the noonday heat, sitting on that bench like a queen on her throne.

As for the vegetables we ate that year—well, never had our garden produced such flavorful abundance. It may have been the weather, the amount of rainfall and such, or it may have been the result of some voodoo magic that Sarimony applied, but more likely those squash and beans just responded to the constant care they received.

As the vegetables began to appear, another surprise unfolded. Sarimony carefully tended her vegetables right up to the moment they were set upon our table. She'd shuck and peel, and then cook up a wonderful dish, with maybe a sprinkling of herbs—one corner of her garden was devoted entirely to herbs. Sometimes she'd put two or three vegetables together in an unusual way, but without fail those concoctions were delicious. Tasting those vegetables, you'd have thought that Sarimony was the most skillful cook around these parts—and yet, mind you, she continued to scorch every chicken she attempted to roast, and her biscuits remained heavy and dry. Her culinary skills, it seemed, applied only to those items that she herself had coaxed from the earth.

I was deeply grateful that the garden experiment turned out well. I was relieved to find *something* favorable about Sarimony, something that I could truly be grateful for. Indeed, that vegetable garden took some of the edge off things, between Sarimony and me.

Chapter Twenty-Two

Wednesday, December 12th, 1860

My dear husband's death draws nearer. As I sit by his bed, I know in my heart that the end is soon and inevitable. Perhaps tonight, perhaps next week. Hope dwindles. Already he lies pale and unmoving. Already the stench fills my nostrils as I lean over him—if not the stench of Death itself, then the smell of sick decay. Not for the past three days, not even for one brief second, has he opened his eyes or acknowledged my presence in any way. Ike is slipping away, beyond my physical grasp—perhaps *has* slipped already, while I sit up here in the dust, trying to revive the warmth of long ago.

I am of two minds these days. Desperately I sit beside my husband, clutching his swollen hand and hearkening to each breath, lest it be his last. I want to cling to him, to share each moment of life that still remains. Yet the tighter I hold Ike's hand, the more I press my cheek against his own, the more I know that he has already departed from me.

And so, when Lydia gently leads me from the room, I do not protest. Instead, I come up here to find my husband. He is with me, my Ike, beneath these eaves. Here, I am alive, and Ike too. I feel his lips against my ear. I hear him whisper...*Dorcas, my blushing beauty.*

It was never my privilege to enjoy the winsome love of springtime. That type of love, I understand, has its own pleasures, but those were not for me. No, my hair had its first silver before I touched a man's body—and *was* touched—beneath a shared counterpane. But I *can* affirm the pleasures and passions that arise in later years. My marriage seemed all the more precious because it occurred so unexpectedly, long after I'd given up hope that I'd ever know such a blessing.

Yet I now sometimes wonder whether I took my good fortune too much for granted, especially during that autumn of Forty-Three. Our household had settled down again after the turmoil of Sarimony's arrival. The garden's success had effected a sort of truce between Sarimony and me. That fall, I vowed to turn more tasks over to Sarimony, though it might mean slackening my standards in some ways. I would not concern myself about the state of our floors, or whether our garments were ironed to complete satisfaction. As far as possible, I would shift the responsibility over to Sarimony. Maybe she would surprise me again. Perhaps, freed from my close supervision, she would show the same initiative that had brought such fine vegetables to our table. Of course, I did not fool myself into thinking that one summer of successful gardening had transformed Sarimony into a perfect household servant. I knew better than that.

Mostly, I vowed to keep my vision fixed upon my own goal: *I would paint, paint, paint.* Wasn't I the mistress, the artist, the instructress? Wasn't Sarimony my servant? Wasn't that Ike's intention?

In September, school resumed. Mrs. Thomas Tucker, now delivered of her child, instructed in needlework, although admittedly there was some debate around town over whether her stitchery could be compared to mine—but I continued to teach drawing and watercolor painting. In that department there was no discussion. My painting received the highest compliments from everyone I knew. My reputation as an artist was growing as rapidly as the town. Indeed, I had heard it boasted more than once, to visitors from elsewhere, that our humble community was quite the cultural equal of any town in the state. Why, just look at the paintings of Mrs. Isaac Howell!

And did I take pride in hearing such boasts, exaggerated though I knew them to be? Yes, I confess to being rather vain about my talents and skills. I was a painter! An artist! I wanted to fill this town with color. New houses were going up, with all those empty walls begging for adornment. If my red silk bonnet grew too snug that autumn, with my foolish head all filled with high-flown notions—well, I was too busy to notice.

For me, that autumn of Forty-Three proved most productive. Ike's children were growing up and did not need all the motherly attention required in previous years. I now had a servant to perform the most tiresome tasks, although naturally I was not entirely free to pursue my art unhampered. Bread still had to be baked, and shirts had to be sewn. I spent part of each morning in tasks of such nature, and two afternoons a week were given to the Tuckers' Female Academy, but the rest of my time could be used to paint. And paint I did.

The novelty of having a likeness taken was rapidly catching hold, and I had more than enough requests to keep me busy. Had there been a photographer in town, Mrs. Dorcas Howell would have found her talents in less demand, but no photographer passed through here, not back then.

My days were more than full, in ways that brought me great satisfaction. If certain matters passed me by, I did not care. You can't pay equal attention to everything at once. I had focused upon a goal and was determined to keep that goal uppermost in mind—after Ike and the children, of course. Besides, I've never been one to pay much heed to gossip. Sometimes a matter has to strike me full in the face before I'm even aware it's there.

When school resumed that autumn, our Dan was not among the Tuckers' pupils. Dan was nineteen that year, a tall and handsome youth. He was slender then, and much resembled his handsome, dark-haired father. Both Dan and his cousin Tom Yancey felt it beneath themselves to sit in a school with younger lads, although, in truth, Dan could not read half so well as his brother Timothy, who was only twelve.

Will Yancey set Tom to reading law, a short-lived experiment, and Ike decided that Dan would work full-time at the store. There were plenty of ways for Dan to be of assistance, although the remuneration was slight, in terms of what Ike could pay. Still, Dan took to storekeeping with a relish. He'd always liked to stand around and talk, and he enjoyed hauling things hither and yon, down to the depot perhaps, or out to some plantation several miles from town. In short, Dan was suddenly a grown man, high-spirited and full of himself.

Our Methodist church here in town was finished that same autumn of Forty-Three, and a big revival was held. Three of Ike's children—Essau, Timothy, and Rachel—were overcome that week with the Lord's salvation. Dan, however, remained unmoved by all the spiritual commotion. Indeed, he missed several of the meetings on some excuse or other. Dan was feeling his oats, testing his limits, like young fellows will do. He began to run about with several rowdy youths, and I suspect they occasionally hoisted a brandy jug, although Dan knew better than to let his daddy find out about that. Ike was a founding member of our new temperance chapter.

Dan also took up swearing. One evening he accosted Sarimony, who was clearing the supper dishes away, with speech that scorched our ears.

"You God-damned black-skinned whore!" Dan said.

Ike immediately rebuked him, of course, and told him plainly that such talk was *not* acceptable. Ike demanded that Dan apologize, which he did. Dan sulked and pouted for a day or two after that, but I never heard him utter those particular words again, at least not in my presence.

In general, my household arrangement seemed to work satisfactorily. Sarimony never achieved perfection or grace, but most of the essential tasks got done. If she was not truly competent, at least she no longer dawdled so obviously. In fact, before long I noticed that our supper was being served promptly each evening, the minute Ike came home from the store, and our plates were whisked away almost before the last bite was taken. Sarimony was anxious to be finished with her evening chores, and who could blame her for that?

When the dishes were back in the cupboard and the kitchen floor was swept, Sarimony was free to spend the remainder of the evening, until curfew, exactly as she wished. I don't mean, of course, that she was at liberty to wander through town, although occasionally she would chat for a while with some of the other Negroes in our neighborhood. But if she wanted to spend an hour stitching a quilt for herself or simply staring into the kitchen fire—well, I did not mind.

Most evenings she went immediately out to her shed. I assumed she was tired and wanted sleep, although occasionally I noticed the flicker of a candle out there, as Ike and I were ready to retire. We allowed Sarimony one candle a fortnight during the wintertime and kept no strict account of the stovewood she used. Her shed was cramped, but the roof was tight, and Ike had installed a rough pine floor and a small iron stove, to make the place suitable for human abode. He had also put in a small window—I was the one who insisted on that, because I could not imagine being cooped up without any of God's natural light.

What did Sarimony have in her cabin? A few spare odds and ends. A cot, a washstand, and a half-dozen pegs in the walls for hanging up aprons and petticoats. I gave her some calico for a curtain, and once when I had carelessly spattered a painting I was working on, she begged me for that half-finished scene. I gave it to her, and also another sketch or two. I suppose she tacked those pictures onto her cabin walls, for the sake of perking up the place, but I don't know. I never stepped foot inside that cabin, once it was occupied.

Sarimony had a natural flair for color, and I counted that in her favor, being myself so partial to bright hues. Gold and orange nasturtiums cascaded around her shed in the summertime. She always wore a bright turban around her head, and on Sundays would tie a matching ribbon around her throat. If I'd given the matter much thought, I might have wondered where she came by such items. I guess I just assumed she had traded a few vegetables for trinkets and such.

One morning, as I came into the kitchen for something, I noticed Sarimony sitting at the table with a far-away look on her face. She was peeling apples, with a wooden bowl in her lap, and I thought to myself: this would make a good painting. I liked the pattern of sunlight across her shoulders, and the bowl nestled among the folds of her apron. I stood in the door for a moment, trying to decide from which angle I'd do the scene, but then Sarimony glanced up and caught my stare. She busied herself again, and I went on to fetch whatever I'd come for.

Two or three weeks after that, on a cold morning in early December, I was upstairs at my easel, finishing a likeness of Judge Keeler's wife and taking particular care with the fringe of her India shawl—Lucretia Keeler was not a handsome woman, but she indulged herself with fine garments. Downstairs, I heard someone knock at the back door, and then caught the drift of voices—Sarimony and someone else, a Negro man, from the sound of things. I did not catch the words, only the flow of speech. I assumed it was a peddler, someone from the country, selling chickens or yams.

In a moment I heard Sarimony on the stairs, coming to ask whether I wanted to buy whatever it was, although I'd told her a dozen times not to bother me when I was painting. But the Sarimony who came to the bedroom door appeared greatly shaken, or ill. At the sight of her, so agitated, I laid my brush aside.

"My mammy be dying," Sarimony said.

I was not prepared for such an utterance. Sarimony's mammy. Did she mean her *mother?* Was there such a person? Indeed, I had given no thought to any kinfolks that Sarimony might have known in her prior existence. She had come into my life alone and complete. I had never even met her previous owners, had never set foot on their place.

And now came this startling news, conveyed third-hand.

"Missy," Sarimony pressed, with a passion I'd seldom seen, "*please* would you ask Mister Isaac to let me walk out yonder, so I can see my mammy again before she passes! I be back by sun-up, I promise, so you folks can eat your victuals on time!"

She leaned forward and for an instant I thought she would actually reach out and clutch my arm.

"Missy, I be *begging* you this!"

So I proceeded to the store and consulted with Ike, who was plenty skeptical. How did we know that message was true, and not simply a ruse? Besides, if her mother was as ill as Sarimony claimed, it made no sense to expose *our* Negro to the same complaint. *And under no circumstances,* Ike asserted, would Sarimony be permitted to traverse the country alone. Then, after he'd voiced all his objections, Ike agreed to send Dan with the wagon, to make certain that Sarimony reached her destination and was safely brought home again.

Sarimony, however, seemed distressed by the prospect of traveling alone with Dan. There was some tension between the two of them—indeed, Dan was more than difficult that year. It surprised me not the least that Sarimony wished to avoid him in her time of grief, so I decided to drive her myself in the carryall. We would stop overnight at the Yanceys' on our return, which would give me a chance to visit with Belle for a while.

By noon we were on our way, and for the next hour or so, Sarimony sat behind me, silent and anxious. Fortunately, we'd had little rain that fall, and the roads were dry, else we might have had to abandon the trip. It was cold, though, and my hands—even in gloves—were aching and stiff before we reached our destination, which appeared to be the middle of nowhere.

Amid fields of stripped cotton stalks sat a low, unpainted house with a verandah across the front. The pale woman who came to greet us, an infant in her arms, seemed surprised at the sight of Sarimony. I was equally surprised when Sarimony ducked her head and called that woman "Missy" in the exact same tone she used with me.

"Well, it's certainly amazing how fast the word can spread, when someone wants it to," the woman said.

With a gesture of her hand, she pointed toward a cluster of sheds that rimmed the bare-dirt yard behind the main house.

"All right," the woman said, "I reckon you can find your way."

Sarimony ran to the furthermost shed and disappeared. The woman, Mrs. Collins, invited me inside to her parlor, and we sat in straight-backed chairs on either side of the hearth, where a blazing fire popped and roared. I was served tea, which warmed my insides again, and we talked politely about children, Negroes, and Christmas. Indeed, I had the distinct impression that Mrs. Collins was hungry for female talk. Her daughters, two frail girls, stood behind their mother and stared at me the entire while. The baby fretted and was handed over to the care of a Negro about the age of our Rachel. Her husband, Mrs. Collins said, was out in his fields, superintending "the niggers."

An hour passed, and the corners of the room grew dim. I knew we had to leave, if we were to reach Belle Yancey's by dark, as I had promised. So I tied on my bonnet once more.

Mrs. Collins followed me across the yard to the furthermost cabin, where I found Sarimony on her knees beside a low cot. The Negro woman lying there was not the withered granny I'd expected, but an older, plumper version of Sarimony herself. I was shocked to learn that Sarimony's mother had not yet reached her thirty-fifth year, eight years younger than me. She was dying of childbed fever, having recently been delivered of her fourteenth child, a strapping boy now given over to the care of another young Negro woman—Sarimony's half-sister, as it turned out.

I felt myself an intruder, standing in the open doorway of that small cabin, an unwilling witness to this scene of grief. I could not help but recall my own times of bereavement—the death of my own dear mother and of my sister Caroline. But it was almost dark, and we had nearly ten miles to go. The sun, like death, cannot be halted on its course.

"Sarimony, I believe it's time," I said.

I expected her to protest and to beg for some few minutes more, but she did not. Instead, she kissed the dying woman, hugged the baby to her breast, and then marched straight out to the carryall.

Sarimony said not a word as we pressed on to Belle Yancey's. Occasionally I thought I heard a high, keening sound, but I was not sure, and I did not look to see.

After our return, Sarimony never again mentioned her mother, nor any other member of her family. Immediately we stepped foot inside this house again, the rhythm of our days resumed, as though they'd never been disturbed, and Sarimony's previous existence was shut tight once more.

And now I must shake away the dust of memory and leave this attic, where twenty years ago seems as sharp and clear as yesterday. Almost with reluctance shall I resume my vigil by Ike's bedside below.

I wonder if Dan is downstairs, and if he's received any replies to the telegraph messages I had him send this morning to Rachel and the other boys: *Best come immediately. There's no more time.*

Chapter Twenty-Three

Thursday, December 13th, 1860

Dan has been by here four or five times already today, for one reason or another, and I think I hear him downstairs again. He's apparently spent all day at the telegraph office, ostensibly checking for replies to his messages of yesterday, but in fact it's the political news that he's eager for. In midafternoon he reported that the Secretary of State has just resigned up to Washington City. He took great satisfaction in announcing the news.

I suspect that Ike's slow demise is of less compelling interest to Dan than all those other doings. Dan is a stout and ordinary man, but he craves excitement. He likes being the first to impart any news. He takes pleasure in evoking astonishment and surprise. Dan's always been like that—and will always be—so there's no use wishing he'd change.

It's not that Dan is bad-hearted. Indeed, he sometimes remind me of an eager, barking hound. His intentions are good, but shallow. Dan is not a person of great moral understanding. He's simply Dan, and I remind myself not to judge him too harshly. Still, I confess that I harbor a certain uneasiness where Dan is concerned, an uneasiness that first developed in that dark-fated spring of Forty-Four.

It was late February when I began to sense that something had shifted within our household. Things were not exactly as they used to be, and yet I could not put my finger on what the difference was. Outwardly, everything was in place, and routines proceeded as before—and yet I perceived a certain tension in the air.

I also began to suspect that I was not *supposed* to know whatever it was. The trail was too carefully covered—or was that merely my imagination? Like every Negro-owner in this state, I suspected thievery or fraud, and I took to watching Sarimony with greater care. I counted our spoons every night, and noted how much coffee, sugar, and tea we had on hand—but, in truth, I could find no evidence there. I also made a great show, for Sarimony's benefit, of inspecting all the cupboards with increased regularity, but Sarimony seemed unconcerned, or else she was mighty clever at masking her alarm.

If not thievery, then what? Did Sarimony neglect her duties and wander about the town, when I was absent from home? But I'd heard no tales, and in a town this size, you're always told promptly whenever your Negro steps out of line. That's something you can count on.

Then one morning, as I was telling Sarimony what to cook for dinner that, I suddenly realized what was wrong: *Sarimony was expecting a child!* Somehow, as I looked at her I knew, though I have never been one of those women who can always "tell" about such matters. The notion struck me with such certainty that I broke off in mid-sentence.

"Tell me, Sarimony," I said, looking her straight in the eye, "Are you in the family way?"

Normally, when I addressed her sternly, Sarimony had a way of ducking her head and avoiding my gaze—hiding from me, despite her physical presence two or three feet away. But this time she did not dodge.

"Don't know, Missy," she replied. "I can't say for sure—but right here lately, I be wondering that same thing myself."

Then she turned and went about her work again, and nothing more was said that day. But for the next week or so, every chance I got, I studied Sarimony—her face, her manner, her form—until I was fairly convinced that my hunch was true. There was a new fullness, a new softness about her. She yawned as she worked, and she ate voraciously, which I took for definite signs.

Who had fathered her child? The question tortured me fiercely. Night and day I worried over that, and I watched Sarimony still more closely, searching for some clue.

It occurred to me that *Dan* might be the guilty one, and once that notion lodged in my mind, I could not shake it free. Little things—a look, a gesture, a word—that had previously passed me by, now carried dark significance. I watched Dan whenever Sarimony was present, and I could not help but acknowledge a carnal gleam in the boy's eye. He'd caught the scent of flesh, that much was clear.

I also observed that Sarimony recognized Dan's attention for what it was. She would avoid his gaze, or place her hand upon her neck, as though to shield herself. At the same time, however, she seemed completely at ease with her womanhood. Her apron could not disguise the sway of her hips, nor the roundness of her bosom.

In fact, Sarimony's clothes had grown snug beyond all modesty. The seams of her dress were strained, so I came up here to this attic and searched in these trunks for one of the full-cut frocks that my sister Caroline had worn when in a similar condition. I took the dress downstairs and gave it to Sarimony, who accepted it with no hesitation.

"Yes'm, I reckon I be needing a dress like this," she said, thus acknowledging what we both knew to be true.

"Sarimony, I wish you would tell me...," I started to say. "What I mean is, how long...?"

But I could not proceed. Some matters are hard to discuss, even between sisters or the closest of friends. Even then, whispers and looks must suffice, because certain things can *never* be spoken aloud. And with a servant, it's yet more impossible. But Sarimony caught the drift.

"Missy, can't tell when," she replied with a shrug. "Maybe this fall...maybe this summer."

"And *who*?"

But Sarimony shook her head and would not reply, which only raised my suspicions the more.

What terrible, terrible days those were for me. The knowledge of Sarimony's condition—and my suspicions as to the father—pierced my self-contentment and threw my life into turmoil. I could no longer paint with concentration. I could not find my usual pleasure in the flowers then edging into bloom. I could not sleep through the night without waking up to worry about what was occurring within my own household.

And did Ike know? Did he have any inkling of what I suspected Dan was up to? One night, under the cloak of darkness, as I lay with Ike in our bed, I brought the matter up, painful though it was.

"Ike," I said, my heart pounding, "I wonder if you've noticed that Sarimony is carrying a child."

"Yes, I've noticed," Ike replied, evenly, showing no surprise. He rolled over, away from me.

"Well, who's the *father*?" I pressed. "There *has* to be a father, and I can't help but wonder...."

"Dorcas, that's *enough*!"

With finality, the door was slammed shut, and I knew better than to push any further. Certain things, in Ike's

154

opinion, are *never, never* to be acknowledged by a white woman. My suspicions were *not* to be voiced.

Ike did not want to know. Or did he *already* know?

Chapter Twenty-Four

Friday, December 14th, 1860

That painful spring of Forty-Four, I gained a new understanding of what it must have been like for Adam and Eve to lose the pleasures of their garden. Once you suspect there's a snake nearby, you can never walk in peace, with your mind at ease. You must always be wary. You must always keep a stick or a hoe at hand and stay alert to the slightest movement or sound. No patch of grass is safe, no flowerbed, no pile of leaves. Every step you take is fraught with anxiety.

That spring, when our garden was plowed, I found no pleasure or relief in watching Sarimony plant her vegetables. Every time something sprouted or another leaf unfurled, I knew we were that much closer to the fateful day of enlightenment. Before the year's harvest, Sarimony's child would be born, an event I did not welcome. What if the child resembled Dan in a way that everyone could see? How could we ever live down the shame of that? No matter what others might acknowledge—or choose not to acknowledge—such a child would be forever a painful sight to me. Could I bear to have in our midst such a reminder of carnal sin? Could I ever again look upon Dan with for-giveness?

This time, I specifically forbade Sarimony the planting of a bean-vine room. There must be no secret place for her to hide. Too late, I honed all my senses. Nothing must escape me, no sight or word. I was wary and alert. I keep track of all comings and goings within our household—not just Sarimony's and Dan's, but Ike's as well, and each of the other children's. Except for my afternoons at the Tucker brothers' school, I did not venture from home myself.

As I worked at my easel, I kept attuned to all voices and sounds down below. Scarcely an hour went by but that I laid my brush aside at least once and went to check on Sarimony's occupation at that precise moment. My painting suffered considerably because I could not focus on my work with a single mind. Always, a part of me was worrying and fretting.

I also took to staying up late at night, after everyone else was in bed—or else getting up again, once Ike had fallen asleep, and fortunately he slept most soundly. While the house was quiet, I watched to see whether all was silent and dark in Sarimony's little shed.

Often Dan stayed out until close to midnight, gone to some frolic. He'd act surprised to see me sitting there, my sewing on my lap, but I think Dan knew I was up on account of him. He'd scowl, and mutter some excuse before going upstairs.

Several times I saw Dan stumbling around in the yard, thrashing through the vegetable garden. I'd watch from the window and see him out there, although I never actually caught him coming from Sarimony's shed.

One night we came to words.

"Why are you always spying on me?" Dan accused. "Why are you always peering out, whenever I go out yonder to relieve myself. I ain't a child, who has to tell his mama whenever he needs to pee."

My actions were unbecoming, I admit. Snooping and spying I've never been one to abide, and yet I could scarcely help myself. After that, I tried to act with greater discretion, but I did not lay my spying aside. Else, things might never have transpired the way they did.

Late one night—it was early May by then—I was awaiting the return of Dan, who had burst out of the house before supper, off to some barbecue. I fear that most of Dan's entertainments bore little resemblance to the singing schools that Ike and I used to attend. Dan ran with a rowdy gang that favored occupations we Methodists frown upon.

Anyway, Ike had long since fallen asleep, and Dan was still out. A wrapper tied over my nightgown, I sat in the dark, keeping my usual vigil. Then, from the back window, as I peered toward the vegetable garden, I saw the door of Sarimony's shed open the slightest bit, and someone slip inside. It happened so fast that I could not tell who it was, but there was sufficient moonlight that I caught the movement.

I stood there watching, all a-tremble, but no one emerged again. I waited for what seemed the longest while. And then, for some unaccountable reason, I decided to set a trap for Dan.

I was barefoot, but I snatched up my black shawl and wrapped myself in that. It was not modesty that led me to cover myself—I wanted a dark disguise that would not catch the moonlight. I stepped outside and, keeping to the shadows, crept furtively toward Sarimony's shed, moving a few inches at a time, one muscle and then the next, careful not to make a sound. I crouched beneath her window, which was ajar. Sheltered by her nasturtium vines, I pressed flat against the rough wood siding.

Fate was with me. No dog barked, and no hen set up a cackle. The locusts continued their songs unabated. The night was warm, and filled with the scent of jasmine. I saw a rabbit hop across the moonlit grass and into the vegetable garden. Insects lit upon my face and arms, but I did not move to slap them away. It was already past midnight as I leaned against that shed, only inches away from Sarimony's cot inside.

I crouched there, listening...and soon I heard, unmistakably, the pantings and sounds of love.

Mortified, I listened to something I had no right to hear. Even in the dark, I could feel my cheeks flush scarlet. I dared not tremble, for fear of being discovered. And thus I heard every sigh and creak until the act was complete.

Then, as I knelt there trying to decide whether to knock upon the shed or merely to sneak away again, I was startled to see Dan himself stumble around the corner of our house. He staggered up the back steps and leaned against a post. Clearly he'd been conversing with Demon Rum and was in a shameful state—*but it was not Dan within the shed!*

I held my breath, hoping against hope that Dan would not look my way, that he would not choose this time to go back of the garden and take care of his private business. I did not want to be discovered, crouching by a Negro's shed, with my nightgown damp from the dew. How could I ever explain myself?

Then, as I watched to see what Dan would do, I grew aware that all was quiet inside the shed as well. It was a watchful silence, not the natural silence of sleep.

Mercifully, after a moment Dan went into the house. Then the whispers began, between Sarimony and some Negro man who I thought to have heard before, but who I could not quite identify. Was it one of Will Yancey's Negroes? Was it Judge Keeler's Cicero? As I searched my brain for who it might be, I realized with a shock *what* they were whispering about: *An escape! Two days hence!*

They were making plans for Sarimony to meet this unseen man sometime after Thursday midnight, at the place where Potter's Mill Road crosses the railroad tracks, four miles north of town.

"Now remember—hold to the shadows," the man was saying. "Stay back to the woods if you can. And keep a sharp watch out for dogs—carry you some biscuit to throw 'em, keep 'em quiet. And, O Lordy, *do* watch out for them paddy-roller men! They nasty mean!"

"How'm I gonna know when I done got to the place where to meet you at?" Sarimony asked. "I ain't never been out that a-way. Ain't never had no reason to go. So how'm I gonna know what road it is?"

"Like I done told you—it be the fifth road across the tracks, once you clear of town. They's a woodshed between two hickory trees, and I be a-laying down flat in the fields behind that shed. But if *you* gets there first, then lay yourself on down and don't get up for nothing, till you hear three hoots of an owl—*whoo, whoo, whoo,* like that. Sugar, you can find the place—you *got* to find it!"

The whispers ceased for a moment, and I heard a murmur, like they might be kissing. I found it strange, such tenderness. They might have been Ike and me.

"What if it be raining?" Sarimony asked, her voice muffled.

"Sugar, pray to Jesus it *don't* rain! Rain'd slow us down a heap. Course, it'd also wash away the smell, and throw off the hounds."

With that, Sarimony began to whimper.

"Sugar, sugar, now don't you cry," he said. "Don't you be a-scared. It'll work out, if we careful."

More comfort, more kisses.

"Say, sugar, you got yourself any shoes?" I heard him ask.

"Yeah, but they hurts my feets pretty bad."

Sarimony did have a pair of shoes, which she wore to church and sometimes on the coldest days. Mostly, though, she went barefoot or wore homemade quilted slippers.

"Bring them shoes anyway," he said. "They'll help keep the blood-suckers off when we be crossing a swamp."

I crouched there, stiff and damp, pressing against that shed and listening to every word. I could hardly contain myself. I was *furious* with Sarimony. How *dare* she plot such a thing?

And yet, at the same time, I felt an enormous relief. Was her Negro lover also the father of her child? Instead of Dan? Desperately I hoped it was so.

After a bit, I heard the shed door open. I was fairly certain that Sarimony's guest would depart the same way he'd come, around the opposite side from where I sat, and indeed that proved the case. I caught no glimpse of him— nor he of me. Then I was free to creep away again.

I had to change my wet nightgown before I slide into bed beside Ike—not to sleep, but merely to rest my bones while I stared into the dark. By the time the first light of dawn appeared and our neighbor's rooster began to crow, I had made up my mind.

Chapter Twenty-Five

Saturday, December 15th, 1860

That Wednesday and that Thursday are sharply etched in my memory. Even at this moment, I can recall with sharp detail every single thing I did, and when, where, and why. Before, all my senses had been attuned to proving my suspicions true. Now, with equal intensity, every thought was geared to *avoiding* suspicion.

Fortunately, ours was a busy family. Ike and the children departed the house about nine each morning and did not return—except for the noon hour—until five. I myself had to spend Thursday afternoon at the Tucker brothers' academy, but every other hour of those two days was spent in preparation.

"Sarimony," I said, almost calmly, on that Wednesday morning as soon as we were alone. "Go out yonder and hitch up the carryall, because I've a notion to go out sketching. And bring yourself a basket, in case we happen upon any wild strawberries."

On some of my landscape expeditions, Sarimony accompanied me, because naturally a lady did not go out sketching in the woods alone. Sarimony usually enjoyed these trips, but that morning she pouted at my request and made it clear that she was in no mood for berry-picking. However, I insisted.

Soon we were proceeding north of town, along the road that follows the railroad tracks. Indeed, shortly after we got under way, the mid-morning train went past, and we had to cover our faces against the soot.

When we reached Potter's Mill Road, I turned and crossed the tracks. There, as I expected, between a pair of well-matched hickories stood a nondescript shed that served as fuel-loading place for the railroad. In fact, a Negro crew was working there that day, stacking wood. As we rode by, I heard a gasp from Sarimony, but I did not slow the horse.

Instead, we continued down Potter's Mill Road raising a cloud of dust behind us. It was my plan to sketch a hasty scene—enough to justify our venture—and then to be home before noon. We entered a stretch of woods, and when we came to a creek, I halted and turned around. Sarimony looked terror-struck, her face ashen gray, as though she'd seen a walking haunt.

"I expect you know what road this is," I said.

"No'm, I ain't got no idea."

In her struggle for composure, Sarimony's voice did not betray her—only the pallor of her face.

"Well, when we head back home, you'd best study those hickory trees—study them good enough to know again in the dark."

Sarimony gave no indication that she knew what I was talking about.

"Missy," she suddenly said, "you reckon they's any strawberries here-about?"

"I'm talking about Thursday midnight," I said.

"Yes'm, I *do* see some berries! Over there!"

She lurched out of the carryall and ran toward the stream. I followed, but I had to grab her arm before she would turn around. What a peculiar pair we made, standing on that creek bank, face to face. Me, a tall white woman—and her, a short pregnant Negro. As we glared at each other, I prayed to heaven there was no one to see us.

"Now, Sarimony, you'd best listen sharp," I said, "because what I'm going to say will never pass my lips again...*but I want you to understand that what's to happen Thursday midnight will occur with my full consent.*"

I was careful, even there in the woods, not to speak above a whisper. It was not easy to convince Sarimony that I meant what I spoke. Why should she trust me? Might it not be a trick? In truth, there was no way to disprove her suspicions, and in the end it had to be her decision—hers and her partner's, whose name she would not divulge.

"What man?" she said. "*Ain't* no man! I don't know no man!"

"Well, you didn't get big by yourself," I insisted, "but never mind—perhaps it's best if I don't know."

I was fairly certain it was one of those Negroes we'd passed at the woodshed, one of the railroad crew, but I pressed Sarimony no more.

Nor would she reveal what route they planned to take, or by what means, or whether it was just the two of them alone. Hence, I could not judge the wisdom of their scheme, although the dangers I well understood. And I also knew there was considerable risk for myself as well, because in these parts we do not take kindly to helping Negroes run away.

That Wednesday afternoon I gave Sarimony a geography lesson. I sketched, to the best of my knowledge, a map of every road in our county and of every town that lay north to Virginia, and then of every city thereafter, all the way to New England. Much of it was hearsay on my part, since I myself had never ventured beyond this state. To-gether, we spent two or three hours going over that map. Sarimony could not read and had not the slightest idea of what "up yonder" was like, or how far things were, but she memorized all the specifics that I thought she should know. Then we burned that map in the kitchen fire.

At my insistence, Sarimony dragged out the washpot, and we dyed one of her petticoats a midnight black, and one of my shawls and a head scarf too. We hung those garments up here in this attic to dry, where no one would see—the drip marks are visible yet, black stains upon this floor. At night, Sarimony could wear those garments and blend into the dark.

Sarimony had already stitched up a pair of pockets to wear beneath her dress. There are certain advantages to being a woman, and a pregnant one at that—no one's likely to ask what's puffing out your skirt. I tried to think of objects that might prove useful in her flight—my sharpest sewing scissors, a pair of Essau's outgrown shoes, a tin container of matches. I even gave her some horehound drops, in case she might be seized by untimely urgings to cough.

How many miles would she have to travel? Would there be someone to provide assistance along the way? Perhaps some distant Quaker cousin of my own? I wrote her a note for my brother James, in case she should pass through Ohio. There was no one else I knew who might be of help. No one at all.

Sarimony had a few coins, saved from Christmastime, hardly enough for two days' provisions. I gave her the twenty-three dollars that I had accumulated from the past year's likeness-painting. Most of that money was intended for canvas and paint, since my supplies were nearly out, and with the rest I'd planned to buy a length of wine-colored silk to make myself a Sunday frock. I tried not to think of that as we wrapped each coin in a separate scrap of paper, so it would not jingle or clink.

I considered, briefly, taking a few dollars from the secret place where I knew that Ike kept his own savings hid. I might have done it, except that Ike has always kept careful track of his money, and there was no predicting when he might decide to count his funds again—perhaps even that Thursday night. I decided against the risk, and as things have since transpired, I've always been grateful that the money I gave Sarimony belonged entirely to me.

Thursday's supper was carefully planned, down to the custard pie. We worked hard at that meal, both Sarimony and me. I wanted Ike and the boys to eat their fill, so they'd sink into ready slumber, and yet I wanted to be certain that midnight indigestion would not disturb anyone.

I worried lest Dan choose that evening to frolic, and lest he not return until the time for Sarimony to depart, but fate proved with us. Dan stayed home that evening, and both he and Ike were engaged in reading the Richmond newspapers brought by train that day. I remember the two of them got into a big discussion, but for the life of me, I cannot recall what it was about. For me, there was only one concern that night.

The windows were open to the scents of May as we sat together in the parlor. The younger boys and Rachel were doing their lessons, and I was making the buttonholes in a shirt for Ike. I remember listening to Timothy practice the speech he was to make at the academy's exercises the following week. I smiled and nodded, and I murmured appreciatively—yet all my attention was elsewhere. At last I heard Sarimony cease sweeping the kitchen floor, and the back of the house grew quiet.

When the clock struck ten, I stood up and yawned conspicuously. Rachel and the younger boys had already gone upstairs. I took Ike's hand and led him to bed. I have never been a woman to take advantage of female wiles, but that night I wanted Ike to feel the urgings of passion, because I knew he'd sleep the sounder for it. And I was not disappointed, yet throughout the familiar motions of love, I remained alert and listening. I was certain that I'd heard Dan go outside.

Ike was soon asleep. I got up to wash myself, then climbed back into bed. Five minutes passed, and five more, as I lay there in the dark, waiting, listening—and praying for the Lord Almighty to send Dan Howell back inside. I wondered if I should go out and search, to shame Dan if need be. I heard the clock strike eleven, and then—merciful heavens—I heard Dan noisily climb the stairs. I heard him pull off his shoes and toss them to the floor. I heard him belch—indeed, not the slightest sound escaped my ears that night.

Beside me, Ike slept on his side, with the sheet drawn up. I was burning hot and could feel myself perspire, but the very next moment I was cold and shivering. I was seized with a sudden need of the chamber pot, but I fought to control myself. I lay there perfectly still, eyes open, and tried to breathe steady, in and out.

I listened for the clock. Midnight came and went. A dog barked, and other dogs answered. Were they sounding an alarm? After a while the barking ceased. I heard the paddy-roller men go by, and a cat began to yowl. Nighttime is quiet, and yet not quiet at all.

Was Sarimony, in her black shawl, now slipping from the shed, bundle in hand? Was her partner already waiting in that field? Or had the plan been changed? Or abandoned? Was there now too much risk—because of *me*?

It was all I could do, to lie there unmoving, when all the while I craved to look out the window—to see for myself whether anything was afoot. Not knowing was a ter-

167

rible strain. The minutes dragged. I may have dozed, but I don't think so.

At one point, seized with the guilt of duplicity, I nearly awakened Ike. I would not have to give the whole plot away. I could merely say that I thought I heard a prowler, out in the yard somewhere. Then Sarimony would be forced to abandon her plan, and I could forget the whole business. No one need ever know, besides Sarimony and me. Our life could continue as before, without upheaval.

In truth, I did turn over and put my hand on Ike's arm, but I could not bring myself to speak his name aloud. I don't know why. I cannot claim it was virtue. I hung in the balance, suspended between fear of what might happen if Sarimony *should* leave...and equal fear of moral embarrassment, should she stay.

That was the longest, hardest night I have ever spent. As I lay there sleepless, I tried to imagine Sarimony and her lover, hurrying through the woods to the north of town. Did they run hand-in-hand?

At length the darkness seemed slightly less intense. I waited until I was sure that the sky had begun to lighten, and then I retrieved from within my pillow a small glass vial that I had previously hidden amid the feathers. Ike still slept as I took a long, deep swallow. I slipped the empty vial back through the slit in the pillow seam and lay down again.

The calomel soon did its work, and most thoroughly, so that by our normal rising time I was leaning over the washbasin and heaving up the remains of last night's supper. In fact, the violence with which that calomel wrung my gut caught me by surprise. My moral quandary was instantly replaced by physical agony.

Indeed I was seized some five or six times, within the space of half an hour, until there was nothing left to come.

Yet still I continued to retch, with dry and painful heaves that gripped my entire body.

Now, Sarimony was no longer my concern. Now, I fought simply to breathe, to lie quiet for a moment without spewing my insides over the bed. I had overdosed myself—but then there'd been no chance for a trial run.

My sudden illness awakened Ike with a shock, and threw him into confusion—all according to my plan. He sprang into action. He wiped my face with a wet cloth, and soon he was hollering for one of the boys to go fetch Sarimony. By then, I felt too ill to care whether they'd find her or not. I did not worry about having to fabricate a lie, because I was so violently ill that I could not speak at all.

That fateful Wednesday and Thursday are still sharp in my mind—but my memory of that Friday morning is mostly one blurred nightmare of trying to hold my guts in place. I began to wonder whether I might actually die. The anxiety, the sleepless nights, and the calomel had all caught up with me.

Eventually, the boys reported that Sarimony could not be found. She was not in her shed, nor in the garden either, and breakfast had not yet been started. The kitchen hearth was cold. As though from far away, I heard the report but was not the least bit interested. Nor was I concerned about how my husband and children would obtain their breakfast. The mere notion of food seemed poison to me.

Somehow, the possibility of Sarimony's complete departure did not occur to Ike, at least not immediately. He was too worried about me. Did I have cholera? Might I die before nightfall?

My dear husband did not leave my bedside all that day—even after Doctor Riggs had examined me and assured Ike that I seemed likely to live. Doctor Riggs was full of the news that one Luke Gates, a black man, had been discovered missing that very morning. Luke belonged to a

Mr. Edward Gates but had been hired out to the railroad to work for wages. He was presumed to have run away.

"That's what happens," the doctor said, "when you give them too much rein. It's bad business, all the way around."

"Is he that smart-talking nigger of Ed's?" Ike asked. "The one that's so strong and hefty?"

"Yes, that's him," the doctor said. "That's Luke. He's got the nick of a scar on his chin."

But I heard no more of that discussion because the potion that Doctor Riggs had given me was finally calming my innards. With relief, I slid into sleep.

Chapter Twenty-Six

Sunday, December 16th, 1860

This house has not contained as many people as it does right now since I can't remember when—probably not since the children have been grown and gone. So much agitation, on top of all we're going through, sets my nerves on edge. Today, even more than usual, I need some time alone so I can settle my thoughts again. Ungracious or not, I had to come up here.

Yet even from this attic I hear the buzz of talk below. You'd think all the noise would rouse up Ike, and maybe that's on folks' minds. Maybe that's what they hope. Ike's children—and they all are in this house today—seem almost to expect that speaking loud will bring their daddy back to his senses.

Sam and Timothy came by train last night, traveling together. Sam works for the railroad, and he offered Timothy some sort of pass, knowing that gospel preachers can't afford normal fares. Timothy is a Methodist preacher, although he confided to me last night that he and Eunice, his wife, are praying that the Lord will call them to China. I hope he knows what he's doing, but then Timothy has always followed his own inner plan. Timothy and Eunice have no children—and no Negroes, either. I praise the Lord for that.

Essau owns a man called Nate, who assists in his store, and I don't know how many Negroes are possessed by Rachel's husband, down to Wilmington. There were eighteen when Rachel married James Beaumont, or so he claimed. Maybe there are more by now, or maybe Mr. Beaumont has lost some of the ones he had. There's no telling what a drinking man will do. Rachel brought her child's mammy along when she arrived this morning on the train from Wilmington, so I assume they're not destitute. Rachel never speaks of her husband's affairs.

I always assumed that Rachel would marry the wealthiest man she could find. That was apparent from her girlhood. From the time she was nine or ten, Rachel made it clear that *she* did not plan to spend her life in household drudgery. Oh, she might make a special cake now and then, or stitch up a fancy gown, but ordinary chores were beneath our Rachel.

The girl suffered mightily from Sarimony's departure. Little Miss Rachel had grown accustomed to putting on airs, like some of the other young ladies at the Tucker brothers' academy, and it was a shock for her to be suddenly thrust back to a servantless state. Rachel resented having to iron her own frock or, worse yet, having to sweep a floor.

For weeks, Rachel refused to believe that Sarimony had permanently disappeared. She would not be convinced. Even after Ike and the others had finally given up hope of Sarimony's return, Rachel continued to believe that the merciful Lord Almighty would hear her prayers and take pity—that He'd send Sarimony back so that she, Rachel, would never have to wash another dish.

Rachel suffered from the loss of Sarimony—but Dan was *outraged*. Lying prostrate in bed that Friday morning,

172

after my foolish dose of calomel, I could hear Dan fume and carry on. From the minute that Doctor Riggs planted the notion that Sarimony might have escaped—and done so in the company of one Luke Gates—Dan could not let it rest. He took Sarimony's departure as a personal affront, which only confirmed my previous suspicions the more.

After the doctor left that Friday morning, Dan saddled the horse and went out searching the countryside. Instead of minding the store, like Ike asked him to, Dan went galloping off in the general direction of the Collins plantation. He didn't return until close to midnight, half inebriated and in the company of young Tom Yancey. I gathered that Dan and Tom had stopped at every house, whether hovel or plantation, but no one had seen Sarimony, or the fellow named Luke Gates. Dan woke Ike and me up to impart this information in a heated, breathless way.

The next morning, Saturday, while Ike continued to stay with me, Dan and Tom set out again, heading towards Smithfield. I don't know why they chose that direction, except that some weeks previous a run-away had been apprehended just off the Smithfield pike. Once more, Dan returned with nothing to show for his venture, other than having spread the word around.

On the third morning, which was Sunday, Ike refused to let Dan have the horse again, on account of it being the Sabbath. Ike wanted all his children to attend church that morning, as a way of showing gratitude to the Lord Almighty for sparing my life. Ike was convinced that only a miracle had saved me from dying of cholera or some other such malady. I was deeply touched by his tender concern—and felt all the more guilty, on account of my own duplicity. Ike's preoccupation with my state of health superseded any plan for action regarding Sarimony's disappearance.

I was still weak that Sabbath afternoon but was at least able to dress and sit for a while in the parlor. By then, several neighbor women had sent over batches of victuals, so that Ike and the children were no longer in danger of starvation. I myself even partook of a little soup.

I was sitting in the parlor when Will Yancey stopped by. He conveyed to me Belle's regards but immediately plunged ahead to his chief concern: Sarimony's escape. I leaned back against my chair and closed my eyes, as though to nap, but every word spoken that afternoon pierced straight into my heart.

"Why didn't you send first thing to borrow my hounds?" Will demanded. "Didn't you have any clothes that belonged to the gal? You should have had those dogs running right away, that very same morning."

"I know it," my husband replied. "I know I should have gotten things rolling immediately—and I should have seen to things myself. But, Will, I couldn't just strike out from home, not knowing if my beloved wife might expire before I got back."

From the respectful silence, I knew they were looking at me, but I did not open my eyes or indicate I had heard a word.

"I *told* him!" Dan burst out. "I told him, sickness or not, we had to get right on it! But does Daddy ever listen to *me*?"

"Well, son," Ike said, "when you've solemnly promised to love, honor, and cherish a woman, then you don't go running off in her hour of need."

My dear husband, put to the test, had sided with *me*. And whose side had *I* been on that Thursday midnight? Which vows had *I* honored?

"All I know is," said Will, "when your money's blowing out the window, you have to grab it quick—else you might never catch it again."

"Will, you're pouring salt in my wounds," Ike said, "and I'm already hurting considerably, just thinking how much I've lost."

The pain in Ike's voice cut me to the quick—a pain that I did not want to acknowledge, yet could not ignore.

"How much exactly *did* you lose?" Will inquired. "If you don't mind me asking."

"Five hundred and fifty," Ike replied, "and most of it still owing. When I got her, I only paid fifty down and signed a note for the rest. And that's not to mention what I've lost on the child she was carrying."

My husband owed hundreds of dollars on a woman who had run away *with my help*. Somehow, in the flurry of the past few days, I had not tallied the cost in this particular way. I, Dorcas Howell, had stolen from my husband the sum of five hundred and fifty dollars. I might as well have set fire to Ike's store, or taken goods from his shelves and thrown them in a river. The net effect was the same. Not only was I guilty of deceit, I had done my husband severe financial harm.

Sarimony had been mine only in intention—not in law. I was not free to let her go. It was not *my* signature upon that note. Now I owed Ike a debt that I would never be able to repay.

I know that you have to *confess* your sin before you can expect forgiveness. I should have confessed to Ike right then, that Sunday afternoon. I should have fully acknowledged my guilt. I should have openly admitted *my* part in Sarimony's escape and told Ike everything I knew: Potter's Mill Road, the woodshed, everything. That would have been the honorable thing to do. My wifely duty was to speak, and then to beg my husband's forgiveness.

But I could not bring myself to say a word. I was mired too deep, beyond any simple extrication. And, I admit it now, I was not entirely willing to face the consequences of my deed, because I was guilty of more than deceit—I had committed an actual crime. When word got out, I would be publicly shunned, if not outright punished. Most especially, I feared Ike's reaction. Would he ever forgive me? Would he ever trust me again, knowing of such treachery?

I am ashamed to say it, but I was too cowardly to speak—not that afternoon or the next day or the next. And still, after all these years, my husband does not know the truth of what occurred that fateful May.

Chapter Twenty-Seven

Monday, December 17th, 1860

Last midnight, while I sat beside Ike's bed, Timothy came in to share my vigil. I found his presence a comfort. Timothy is more inclined to somber contemplation than Ike's other children, and he's not so readily distracted by the news from South Carolina. It's not that I blame the other boys, or Rachel either. These are times of terrible upheaval, what with Ike's imminent passing, and then that convention occurring down to Columbia—or rather, down to Charleston. The convention has been moved, on account of the smallpox.

These are such wild, strange days that I would not be surprised to feel the earth start shaking beneath my feet. I doubt I'd even blink if a whirlwind were to lift the roof of this house and shatter these walls into splinters. I half expect such a calamity, but in the meantime—like my dear Isaac—I shut my eyes and ears to the fury that blows around us. I try to cling to my sanity—and to Ike, and to the past we have shared.

Timothy did not engage me last night in political talk. He's used to keeping watch beside the dying, because that's what preachers do. Preachers also know about the weight of sin.

I came close last night to speaking with Timothy about this matter that presses upon my soul. In the end, I held my tongue. Perhaps it was stiff-necked pride that kept me from confessing to Ike's son. Mostly, though, it seemed unkind to thrust my personal burdens upon young Timothy, in this time of sorrow, when he is here to be with his dying father. Timothy has his own memories to recall.

Besides, I was not entirely certain how Timothy would judge the matter of Sarimony. Could he be impartial about an event that occurred in his childhood? It seemed best to let sleeping dogs lie.

So Timothy sat with me, reciting Scripture from memory and praying at length on Ike's behalf. He also talked about far-off China, and why he hopes to be summoned there. I listened and nodded, and spoke not a single word about what concerns me most.

Back in the spring of Forty-Four, when I assisted in Sarimony's departure, I thought I was putting an end to a grievous situation that threatened my family's harmony. I thought I was taking steps to keep our happiness intact. If I could have foreseen the future, I might not have been so rash. Maybe it's a blessing we cannot see our fate, else we couldn't abide it.

By Monday morning after Sarimony's departure, I was back on duty in our kitchen. My respite from household chores, enjoyed for the past sixteen months, had come abruptly to an end. I was still terribly weak, and the notion of food still set my stomach a-quiver, but I was determined that Ike would have his accustomed breakfast: fried eggs, side meat, and hoe cake.

I vowed that my husband would never suffer physical discomfort on account of Sarimony's departure. Meals would be served on time, and clothes would be laundered with the usual regularity. I tied on my apron, rolled up my sleeves, and set to work. Admittedly, I found little joy in the task. Drudgery is not pleasurable, but our changed circumstances—as I painfully knew—were largely of my own doing. I had no right to complain.

That morning, Ike lingered at the breakfast table, drinking a second cup of coffee, while I cleared the dishes away. Perhaps I frowned in my haste. Certainly my illness had left me pale and gaunt, and I guess that Ike was studying me.

"Oh, my dear wife!" Ike suddenly exclaimed. "The absolute *worst* of this is seeing you labor so, after all my intentions to free you for better things. I declare, if I had the money, I'd start looking for a girl all over again."

"What? You'd buy *another* one—to run away too?"

Anguish passed over my husband's face, and immediately I wished I had not replied in such a way.

"No," Ike said, "I reckon I've learned *that* lesson pretty well—and anyway, it's not likely I'll ever have the money again, not now. But, Dorcas, that doesn't help you any."

I quickly turned away, lest Ike see my tears. *He* was the one apologizing, and I couldn't bear it.

Cowardice had silenced me but left a strong craving for penance. I had sinned against my dear husband, and I yearned to make retribution. It's not that I wanted Sarimony enslaved again—far from it!—but I wanted to make things honest and right once more between Ike and myself. Had I read Mr. Hawthorne's tale, I might have devised some symbol to wear upon my breast, but it was not until some years later that Mr. Hawthorne's book appeared. I had no hidden emblem to signify my repentance, no amulet to draw away the pain. My suffering—and I suffered mightily—remained private and unshared.

Laying my paints aside was not initially an act of penance. I was too busy with running the household and could not spare the easel time I'd grown accustomed to. Then, when I did take up my brush again, expecting to finish a likeness I'd started some weeks before, the brush seemed to burn my hand. No matter how hard I tried, I could not seem to paint with any satisfaction. How dare I, Dorcas Howell, stand there in fruitful creation, knowing what I'd done to my husband? How dare I mix my bright colors and dab them on a canvas, in the light of all that had recently transpired?

Though I made several attempts at resuming my work, I gradually came to understand that my life as an artist had ended. I could not pretend that things were the same as before—or that *I* was the same. Somehow, to compensate for what I'd done, I felt that I had to relinquish something that I cherished, something that really mattered to me. I must give up my painting. It was the least I could do.

And so one morning when I was home alone, I came up here to this attic and packed away all my painting paraphernalia—sketchbooks, brushes, canvas, and the like. I nailed the crate shut and pushed it under the eaves, there in that corner. Admittedly, I shed some tears before I went downstairs again. And many's the time, over the years, that I have been tempted to rip that crate open again, simply to feel the weight of a brush in my hand, to smell the pungency of turpentine and linseed oil—but always I have desisted. My sacrifice has lessened my guilt not one whit, but it was something I had to do.

Several times that summer of Forty-Four, Ike remarked that he hadn't noticed me painting for quite some while.

"Oh, I haven't the spirit for painting these days," I replied, keeping my voice calm.

Ike did not press the matter. I expect he assumed it was another consequence of that sudden illness I'd experienced in May. Indeed, if the truth be known, I rather encouraged

Ike to view that illness as the cause of all the changes I'd undergone.

After that, whenever folks asked me to paint their likeness, I politely declined. Soon, folks stopped asking, and it came to be understood that Dorcas Howell did not paint anymore.

But giving up my paints was nothing compared to the painful damage that my deeds had wrought upon Ike and me, because from that May onward, things were never quite the same between us. It's not that we fought and disputed, or that our outward manner changed, but somehow we began to drift apart, flowing down separate streams. Although we continued to dwell together beneath one roof, and slept beside each other in one bed, a deep silence developed between us, an ever-widening gulf of heart and mind. We lost the close affection we once had known.

I alone bear the blame for this. My guilt was too overpowering. My reluctance to *truly* speak kept me from breaking the silence, from bridging the gulf. In subtle ways, I began to hide from my husband, lest by a slip of the tongue I betray myself and thus lose Ike's love completely.

The events of that fateful May left a sad legacy—and gave no satisfaction in return, because when Sarimony stole away, she vanished totally from my sight. For months afterward, I was obsessed with Sarimony and her whereabouts. I would lie awake in the night, trying to imagine where she was at that moment. Had she reached the safety of Boston? Or Canada? Or had she been captured along the way, and sold into bondage again? Was she lawfully married now to Luke Gates? Had the child been born? Had it survived? And was it mulatto, or black?

Unlike the novels of Mrs. Stowe, the story of Sarimony has never been written to a proper conclusion. No word ever came about Sarimony or her man. They had completely disappeared. And *not* knowing has added to my burden.

The deceit I carry in my heart has grown less sharp-edged over the years, but it's always there, jabbing me, no matter which way I move. My sin has not been absolved. Even now, on the eve of Ike's passing, my treachery divides my dear husband and me.

Oh, Ike, I beg your forgiveness! Oh, Ike, come back to me!

Chapter Twenty-Eight

Thursday, December 20th, 1860

My beloved husband was laid to rest this day. I have tried, over the past weeks, to prepare myself for this shock, but imagined pain does not equal the suffering that comes from watching your own dear husband breathe his last, or from hearing the thud of clay upon his final resting-box. Ike is gone. His agony has ceased, but mine goes on.

The burial was at half past ten, between the passing of the morning trains, so the clamor would not interrupt our pondering of the journey that Ike has embarked upon. Ike would have been pleased to see such a gathering, but I'm not entirely sure that everyone who came was there strictly on account of Ike. People seemed eager to cluster together. Even in the act of mourning, an undercurrent of excitement rippled the crowd that was standing about Ike's grave. Whispers and looks were exchanged. Nerves were on edge, and voices rose to an unnatural pitch. The news from Charleston is making folks restless.

After the burial was over, we came back here for the funeral repast. When the meal was over, Ike's children gathered in the parlor to discuss what ought to be done with everything. Certain spiritual matters have moved beyond our reach, but Ike's earthly possessions remain.

Every so often, despite the discussion, Dan would lift his head as though listening for a signal.

"I wonder if there's been any word from Charleston yet," he would say.

I sat there as long as I could, but at length I excused myself to come up here to this attic again. One final time, I want to sit amid these shadows and memories. Tomorrow morning, early, these trunks and crates will all be opened, and their contents sorted through, with the leavings of the past held up for everyone to see. Faded frocks will be unfolded, and letters read. Even so, certain past events will not be revealed. No one will notice the stains on this attic floor, left from a black-dyed petticoat hanging up here to dry.

With Ike's passing, this house will not be the same. Indeed, I already feel the change.

But why is there so much noise outside? Why are church bells ringing? Could it be the news from Charleston that everyone's been waiting for?

Acknowledgments

The seed money for The Days & Years Press came from the estate of my father, Robert Lee Hardison, who died November 2, 1993, a week short of his eightieth birthday. My father was a man without pretensions, a man of deep Christian faith, and—when necessary—a man of moral courage. His true love was gardening—vegetables mostly, but also flowers and fruit. He was always happy when nurturing his plants, grinding up leaves to enrich the soil, or harvesting and eating his produce. And he was generous with the fruits of his labor, often giving away seedlings or vine-ripened vegetables.

I like to think that writing and reading are like gardening in a way, because ideas, images, and phrases bear fruit in unexpected ways. We may start out planting the words in neat, even rows, but then a volunteer springs up outside the border and offers some new insight. Or a cutting gets passed from hand to hand and eventually grows into a beautiful shrub in some stranger's backyard, in a place and form far beyond our initial imagining.

Several years before I started writing *I Shall Never Speak*, I ran across *Antebellum North Carolina*, by the late Dr. Guion Griffis Johnson, in the public library of Oakland, California. *Antebellum North Carolina*, one of the first "social histories," describes the everyday life and customs of ordinary North Carolina people in the decades before the Civil

War and has been an invaluable resource. I was later privileged to meet Dr. Guion Johnson and her husband, the late Dr. Guy B. Johnson, a sociologist, and to spend several sparkling hours with the two of them, enjoying their wit and their observations about North Carolina.

On trips to Chapel Hill to visit my family, I also spent many useful hours in the University of North Carolina's Louis R. Wilson Library, where the North Carolina Collection revealed many treasures, such as an 1825 map of Fayetteville and contemporary newspaper accounts of Lafayette's visit and of the 1831 fire.

The library at the University of California, Berkeley, helped fill numerous gaps in my research, with books on American folk art, General Lafayette, and Southern history and with antebellum newspapers from Charleston, South Carolina, and Richmond, Virginia. Much of this novel was written, in longhand, at one of the long oak tables in the reference room of the Main Library.

I Shall Never Speak was completed in 1985 and has had only minor textual editing since then.

G.V.K.

Gina V. Kaiper grew up in Chapel Hill, North Carolina, and graduated from the University of North Carolina. In the late 1960s, she moved to the San Francisco Bay Area. She now lives in Pleasanton, California, and earns her living writing about science and technology.